Dear Reader,

For the past twenty years Silhouette has been bringing you stories of love, laughter, passion and families. I have been honored to be a part of that tradition for more than half of that time. I can't imagine anything more rewarding, either as a writer or as a reader. In the end, you see, that is what I am—a reader, just like you.

I love to read about that first hesitant glance of interest between two people, about their struggles to make a relationship work and, of course, about the power of love. As a former journalist who still avidly follows the news, I know that the world is often not a pretty place, just as the path to love is not always smooth. But I am ultimately a believer in the happy ending, and nobody brings you that with more variety, more tears, more laughter and more satisfaction than Silhouette. I'm so glad to be a part of that tradition and even more delighted that you are, too.

With warm congratulations to Silhouette for bringing a little touch of romance into all of our lives.

Sheryl Woods

* * *

And Baby Makes Three:
The Delacourts of Texas:
A Delacourt of Texas finds love, and fatherhood, in a most unexpected way!

Dear Reader,

With spring just around the corner, Silhouette's yearlong 20th Anniversary celebration marches on as we continue to bring you the best and brightest stars and the most compelling stories ever in Special Edition!

Top author Sherryl Woods kicks off the month with *Dylan and the Baby Doctor,* a riveting secret baby story in the next installment of AND BABY MAKES THREE: THE DELACOURTS OF TEXAS.

From beloved author Marie Ferrarella, you'll love *Found: His Perfect Wife,* an emotional story in which a man loses his memory and gains a temporary spouse.... And reader favorite Victoria Pade continues her popular cowboy series A RANCHING FAMILY with *Cowboy's Caress,* a heartwarming story about a woman who's ready to travel the world—until love comes to town!

Millionaire's Instant Baby is rising star Allison Leigh's must-read contribution to the series SO MANY BABIES. In this provocative story, a dashing tycoon gets more than he bargained for when he hires a single mom as his pretend wife in order to close a business deal.

THE BLACKWELL BROTHERS continue to capture hearts in the next book of Sharon De Vita's cross-line series. In *The Marriage Promise,* a Blackwell brother is determined to woo and win the forbidden love of a beautiful Amish virgin. And you won't want to miss *Good Morning, Stranger,* Laurie Campbell's dramatically poignant story about a woman, a child and a handsome, mysterious stranger who uncover secrets that bring together a meant-to-be family.

It's a month chock-full of great reading and terrific variety, and we hope you enjoy all the stories!

All the best,
Karen Taylor Richman
Senior Editor

Please address questions and book requests to:
Silhouette Reader Service
U.S.: 3010 Walden Ave., P.O. Box 1325, Buffalo, NY 14269
Canadian: P.O. Box 609, Fort Erie, Ont. L2A 5X3

SHERRYL WOODS

DYLAN AND THE BABY DOCTOR

SPECIAL EDITION®

Published by Silhouette Books
America's Publisher of Contemporary Romance

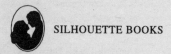 SILHOUETTE BOOKS

ISBN 0-373-24309-X

DYLAN AND THE BABY DOCTOR

Copyright © 2000 by Sherryl Woods

This edition published by arrangement with Harlequin Books S.A.

® and TM are trademarks of Harlequin Books S.A., used under license.
Trademarks indicated with ® are registered in the United States Patent
and Trademark Office, the Canadian Trade Marks Office and in other
countries.

Visit us at www.romance.net

Printed in U.S.A.

SHERRYL WOODS

Whether she's living in California, Florida or Virginia, Sherryl Woods always makes her home by the sea. A walk on the beach, the sound of waves, the smell of the salt air all provide inspiration for this writer of more than sixty romance and mystery novels. Sherryl hopes you're enjoying these latest entries in the AND BABY MAKES THREE series for Silhouette Special Edition. You can write to Sherryl or—from April through December—stop by and meet her at her bookstore, Potomac Sunrise, 308 Washington Avenue, Colonial Beach, VA 22443.

IT'S OUR 20th ANNIVERSARY!
We'll be celebrating all year,
continuing with these fabulous titles,
on sale in March 2000.

Special Edition

#1309 Dylan and the Baby Doctor
Sherryl Woods

#1310 Found: His Perfect Wife
Marie Ferrarella

#1311 Cowboy's Caress
Victoria Pade

#1312 Millionaire's Instant Baby
Allison Leigh

#1313 The Marriage Promise
Sharon De Vita

#1314 Good Morning, Stranger
Laurie Campbell

Intimate Moments

#991 Get Lucky
Suzanne Brockmann

#992 A Ranching Man
Linda Turner

#993 Just a Wedding Away
Monica McLean

#994 Accidental Father
Lauren Nichols

#995 Saving Grace
RaeAnne Thayne

#996 The Long Hot Summer
Wendy Rosnau

Romance

#1432 A Royal Masquerade
Arlene James

#1433 Oh, Babies!
Susan Meier

#1434 Just the Man She Needed
Karen Rose Smith

#1435 The Baby Magnet
Terry Essig

#1436 Callie, Get Your Groom
Julianna Morris

#1437 What the Cowboy Prescribes...
Mary Starleigh

Desire

#1279 A Cowboy's Secret
Anne McAllister

#1280 The Doctor Wore Spurs
Leanne Banks

#1281 A Whole Lot of Love
Justine Davis

#1282 The Earl Takes a Bride
Kathryn Jensen

#1283 The Pregnant Virgin
Anne Eames

#1284 Marriage for Sale
Carol Devine

Prologue

A half dozen yelling, laughing toddlers raced around the backyard of pediatrician Kelsey James. They were definitely on a sugar high after consuming enough birthday cake and ice cream for twice as many kids.

Maybe they hadn't actually consumed it, she concluded after a survey of the mess. An awful lot appeared to have been smeared over shirts, spilled on the dark green picnic table or dumped in the grass, along with trails of ribbon and shredded wrapping paper. Melting pools of vanilla ice cream were everywhere. Having the party outside had been a very smart decision.

"Obviously, the party is a success," Lizzy Adams-Robbins declared, conducting her own survey of the damage. "I can't imagine why you were so worried."

Finally, after days of ridiculous anxiety over throwing a kid's birthday party, Kelsey actually allowed herself to relax. She listened to the laughter and smiled for the first time in days, maybe longer. The tight knot in her stomach eased and something that felt a lot like contentment replaced it. It was such a fragile, unfamiliar sensation, she basked in it for just a moment before responding.

"It is wonderful, isn't it?" she said finally. "I know I was acting like a nutcase over this, but Bobby's been through so much these past few months—leaving his dad, moving to a new place, making new friends. I just wanted his birthday party to be special. The Western theme was his idea. Ever since we stayed out at your father's ranch, he's really taken with the idea of being a cowboy."

"Well, the new boots were definitely a big hit," Lizzy said.

"They ought to be. Custom boots for a three-year-old." Kelsey shook her head. "I must be overcompensating."

Lizzy, whom she had known since med school in Miami, squeezed her hand. "Kelsey, stop with the guilt this instant. You had no choice. You had to divorce Paul. He was a creep. And you were absolutely right to get out of Miami and come here. The clinic needed you. I needed you. And Bobby is fitting in just fine." She clasped Kelsey's shoulders and turned her to look at the chaos. "You can stop overcompensating. Does that look like a little boy who is unhappy?"

Kelsey found herself grinning again at the sight of her son, his chubby little legs pumping furiously to keep up with the older children, his face streaked with chocolate frosting and vanilla ice cream. He looked like a perfectly normal little boy who was having the time of his life.

"He is having a good time, isn't he? And the presents…" She shook her head in bemusement. "Your family really didn't have to go crazy with the presents. There are too many toys. He doesn't play with even half of the ones he has now."

Lizzy rolled her eyes. "Tell that to my father. He doesn't believe it's possible for a child to have too many toys. Nothing makes him happier than spoiling his babies, and as far as he's concerned you and Bobby became part of the family the minute you arrived in town."

Harlan Adams truly was remarkable. Kelsey had heard all about him from Lizzy, of course, but even all those old tales of a doting father hadn't prepared her for the incredible eighty-nine-year-old patriarch of the Adams clan. She had never known anyone as generous or as wise. Or as meddlesome, she thought fondly.

When he'd first heard about Kelsey's decision to leave Miami and the reasons for it, he'd called her himself and added his invitation to Lizzy's. Once she was in Los Piños, he'd welcomed her warmly, taking her and Bobby into his own home at White Pines until they could find a place of their own. He'd allowed the two of them to leave only when he'd checked out the new house for himself and concluded that it was suitable. He'd even insisted she raid his attic for furniture, since she'd taken very little from the Miami home she had shared with Paul.

Harlan Adams had also extracted a promise that they would go on joining the family for Sunday dinner at the ranch. He was as indulgent and attentive with Bobby as he was with all of his own grandchildren and great-grandchildren. Bobby had basked in the masculine attention, a commodity that had been all too rare in his young life. His own father had been too busy scoring business deals and pills to pay much attention to him.

With her own parents far away in Maine and not nearly as generous with their love or their time, Kelsey was more grateful for the Adamses than she could ever say. She owed them all, but especially Harlan, his wife Janet, and of course Lizzy, the best friend any woman could ask for. Lizzy had made it all possible and acted as if Kelsey were the one doing her a favor, rather than the other way around.

"Have I told you how grateful I am?" she asked Lizzy.

"Only about a million times," Lizzy said. "I'm the one who's grateful. We needed a pediatrician here and I can't imagine anyone I'd rather work with than you. The timing couldn't have been better."

"Still—"

"Stop it," Lizzy said firmly. She studied Kelsey intently. "Are you really doing okay, though? No second thoughts? No regrets over divorcing Paul? Los Piños is a far cry from Miami and our little clinic would fit into one tiny corner of the trauma center back there."

"Definitely no regrets over Paul. And you were the one who was hell-bent on being a big trauma doctor. I just love kids. It doesn't matter where I treat them. I couldn't be happier right here," Kelsey reassured her, meaning every word.

The differences were all good ones. There was a sense of community here that was never possible in a bustling, urban environment like Miami. While she might have made a difference in Miami and while the medical challenges might have been greater, here the rewards came in the form of sticky hugs from her pint-sized patients and warm, grateful smiles from people she was getting to know as friends.

Most of all, Los Piños was far away from Paul James and the disaster he had almost made of both their lives. Hopefully, he would never discover her whereabouts. Hopefully, her ex-husband would forget her existence—and Bobby's. That was the deal they had made. She would forget his deceit, his illegal use of her prescription pads to get narcotics, and he would leave her and his son alone.

Forgetting hadn't been easy. At the end, Paul's behavior had been so erratic, so unpredictable, she hadn't been convinced he would stick to his word…or even remember he'd given it. It had been nearly a year now, and so far she hadn't heard so much as a peep from him. She was finally beginning to relax her guard a little. She'd stopped panicking whenever the phone rang or whenever a strange car drove past the house.

She glanced at Bobby, who was adding grape juice to the stains on his face and clothes, and smiled. He was all boy, a miniature version of her ex, with the same dimpled smile, the same light brown hair and dark brown eyes. But while her son's eyes were bright and clear and most often twinkling with laughter, Paul's had been shadowed or too-bright with the drugs she hadn't guessed he was taking until way too late.

She felt Lizzy squeeze her hand, looked up and met her friend's concerned gaze.

"Don't go back there," Lizzy advised. "Not even for a minute. You couldn't have changed anything. It was Paul's problem, not yours. If he didn't care enough about himself or you to get off the pills, nothing you could have done would have helped."

Kelsey was amazed by Lizzy's perceptiveness. "How did you know what was on my mind?"

"Because it usually is. Besides, I always know what you're thinking, just the way you could read my mind back in med school. You knew how I felt about marrying Hank practically before I did."

Kelsey chuckled. "Not possible. You knew you were in love with Hank Robbins from the time you were a schoolgirl. From the moment we became roommates, all I ever heard about was Hank this or Hank that. It didn't require major deductive reasoning to figure out you were crazy about the guy."

"I knew I was in love with him, yes, but not that I was ready to marry him and juggle a baby, marriage and med school," Lizzy said. "I was scared silly when I found out I was pregnant. You helped me to see that I had to take that final leap of faith, that we could make it work."

Lizzy wasn't exaggerating her panic. Kelsey recalled exactly how upset Lizzy had been when she'd first realized she was pregnant with Hank's baby. There had never been a doubt in Kelsey's mind what the outcome would be, especially once Hank had found out about the pregnancy. Lizzy's handsome, totally smitten cowboy had pursued her with relentless determination, ignoring her doubts, finding solutions and compromises that Lizzy had claimed were impossible.

"It's worked out fine, hasn't it? No regrets?"

"Better than fine, smarty." Lizzy grinned, then leaned closer to confide in a whisper, "In fact, we're going to have another baby."

"Oh, my." Kelsey sighed, trying to hide any hint of envy. She had wanted a whole houseful of kids herself, but if Bobby was all she ever had, he would be enough. She gave Lizzy a fierce hug. "Congratulations! That's wonderful. Does Hank know yet?"

Lizzy gave her a rueful look. "You may have found out before he did last time, but this time I thought Hank ought to be the first to know. I told him last night."

"And?"

"He's over the moon. He's wanted this for a long time. I was the holdout. While I was finishing my residency and getting the clinic started, I didn't think he should carry all the burden for child care, even though he seems to love it. I figured it was about time I pitched in, too. The clinic's hours are a whole lot more consistent than my hours at the hospital in Garden City. I might actually get to see this baby's first step and hear his or her first word. I missed so much of that with Jamey."

"I am so happy for you."

"Will you be a godmother to this one?"

Kelsey was enchanted with the idea of becoming an even more integral part of the extended Adams family. "Nothing would please me more," she said at once. "Of course, with the two of us to influence this baby, he or she won't have any choice but to be a doctor."

Lizzy shook her head. "Not a chance. Girl or boy, Hank wants a rancher. He says Jamey already spends too much time wanting to cut up frogs like his mama did in school."

Lizzy glanced around at the half dozen kids, most of whom were beginning to fade from all the partying. Her gaze sought out Jamey, who was tanned and had his daddy's rich brown, sun-streaked hair. He was five now and had a definite mind of his own. The stubborn streak was Lizzy's contribution, according to Hank, along with the fascination with cutting up dead critters.

"Well, I think it's time to get the troops home before they all wind up sound asleep in your backyard," Lizzy said.

"Thank you again for helping today," Kelsey said.

"Anytime. If you need any of us for anything ever, all you need to do is call. Day or night, okay?"

It was something Lizzy never failed to remind her of, Kelsey thought, as her friend left with a carload of exhausted Adams kids. Although she appreciated the gesture of support, too often it only served as an unnerving reminder to Kelsey that as unpredictable as Paul James was, there very well could come a time when she would desperately need their help.

Chapter One

Dylan Delacourt knew perfectly well why he'd been spending so much time visiting his baby sister lately. Oh, he claimed that he was just checking up on her for the rest of the family. He said he liked helping his new brother-in-law work on the house Hardy had built for Trish. But the truth was, he was in Los Piños because of his niece.

Baby Laura had stolen his heart. On his worst days, when he was so low everything looked black, Laura's smile was like sunshine. Seeing it was a bittersweet sensation, though. It reminded him just a little too much of another baby, another sweet smile.

The last time he'd held his son, Shane had been just about Laura's age, thirteen months. He'd just begun to toddle around on unsteady legs. He'd uttered his first word, *Mama,* and that had pretty much been the moment when Dylan had concluded that Shane belonged with Kit and her new husband full-time.

Saying goodbye to his boy, doing what was best for him and letting him grow up with a ''father,'' rather than a stepfather, had almost killed Dylan. He'd agonized over it for months, hated Kit for divorcing him and forcing him into making such an untenable decision.

But he had also known just how deep the bitterness between him and Kit ran, recognized that no matter how hard they tried, there would never be agreement or peace or cooperation between them. In the end, he hadn't been willing to subject his son to the inevitable battles, the simmering resentments. Giving up Shane was probably the single most unselfish act of his life. And not a day went by that he didn't regret it.

His own grief and pain had been lessened somewhat by the knowledge that Kit's new husband was a kind, decent man, who already had two boys of his own. Steve Davis kept regular hours, not the erratic, unpredictable schedule of a private eye. He would give Shane the time, the love and the whole family that the boy deserved.

Dylan tried never to look back, but there were too many days and twice as many nights when that was impossible. It had been more than four years now and he still ached for his boy. He wondered how tall he was, if he still had the same cowlick in his hair, if he was athletic, if he remembered his real daddy at all. That's when the regrets would start to add up and he'd turn up in Los Piños, his mood bleak, his soul weary.

Trish intuitively understood what brought him there and over time, Dylan had revealed some of it to Hardy. He withstood their pitying looks, accepted their love and their concern. But with little Laura, there was only the sunshine of her brilliant smile and the joy of her laughter. He could be a hero, instead of the dad who'd walked away.

"Unca Dyl," she squealed when she saw him climb out of his rugged sports utility vehicle on a dreary Friday night. Arms outstretched, she pumped her little legs so fast, she almost tripped over her own feet trying to get to him.

Dylan scooped her up and into the air above his head until she chortled with glee. He brought her down to peer into her laughing blue eyes that were so like her mama's. He'd been nine when Trish was born and he could still remember the way she, too, had looked up at him as if he were ten feet tall.

"Munchkin, I think you're destined to be a pilot or an astronaut," he declared. "You have absolutely no fear of heights."

Laura giggled and gestured until he lifted her high again, then swung her low in a stomach-sinking dip.

"Still making career choices for her, I see," Trish said, stepping off the porch to join them. "For a man who refused to let anyone tell him what he should grow up to be, you seem intent on controlling your niece's destiny."

"Not controlling it," Dylan insisted. "Just listing a few of her options." He dropped a kiss on his sister's cheek. "Thanks for letting me come."

Instantly, sympathy filled her eyes. "I know it's a tough weekend. Shane will be six tomorrow, right?"

Dylan nodded. "I don't want to talk about it, though."

Trish sighed. "You never do. Dylan, don't you think—"

"I'm not going to get in touch with him," he said fiercely. "I made a deal with Kit and Steve. I intend to stick to it. If the time ever comes when Shane wants to know me, she'll help him find me. Until then, I have to forget about him."

"I don't know how you can live with that," she whispered, touching his cheek. "I know you think it was the right thing to do, but—"

"It was the only thing to do. Now can we drop it, please? I could have stayed home and listened to Mother, if I'd wanted to go over this again. Goodness knows, she never lets me forget how I'd deprived her of getting to know her first grandchild."

Trish looked as if she might argue, then sighed. "Done. I hope you're hungry, though. Hardy's out back making hamburgers on the grill. It's his night to cook and if it can't be done on a grill, we don't eat."

Over the weekend, Dylan fell into the easy rhythms of his sister's family, grateful to be able to push the memories away for a few days at least. When Sunday rolled around, he still wasn't ready to go back to Houston and face real life. None of the cases on his desk were challenging. Just routine skip-traces, a straying husband, an amateur attempt at insurance fraud. He could wrap any one of them up in less than a day, which was one of the reasons he'd been so desperate to get away. Tackling them wouldn't have crowded out his misery.

"Stay one more night," Trish begged.

He figured she'd sensed his reluctance to go. His baby sister had always been able to read him like a book, better than any of the younger brothers who'd come between them. Fiercely loyal and kindhearted, the male Delacourts taunted each other and banded together against the outside world. But as tight-knit as they were, none of his brothers dared to bulldoze through his defenses the way Trish did.

"Yeah," Hardy agreed, picking up on some unspoken signal from his wife. "Stick around. You can get the tile up in the second bathroom. Trish says I don't have the patience to do it right."

"And I do?" Dylan said, amused by their ploy to make him feel that his continued presence wasn't an intrusion. Crediting him with more patience than anyone was a real stretch.

"Trust me," Trish said. "You're bound to have more than my husband. He keeps getting distracted."

Hardy grinned. "Because I happen to have a very sexy new wife."

Sometimes witnessing their happiness was more painful than going back to his lonely existence in Houston, but tonight there was no contest. Anything was better than going home.

Dylan held up his hands. "Okay, okay, no details, please. You two may be married, but she's still my baby sister. I'll stay."

"Good," Trish said, beaming, clearly pleased with herself.

That night, just as they were finishing supper, the phone rang. Because he was closest, Dylan grabbed it.

"Oh, Dylan, is that you?" a vaguely familiar voice demanded.

Dylan tensed, alerted by the tone to trouble. "Yes. Who is this?"

"It's Lizzy. Lizzy Adams. I'm the doctor who treated Trish after Laura was born. We met at Trish's wedding."

He recalled a slender, dark-haired woman who'd radiated confidence. She didn't sound so sure of herself now. "Of course. You want to talk to Trish. She's right here."

"No, no. It's you I need to speak to."

"Oh?"

"You're a private detective, right?"

"Yes." He slid into professional mode, finally grasping that what he was hearing in her voice was a thread of panic she was trying hard to hide. "What's going on?"

"My friend, the doctor who works with me at the clinic, Kelsey James...have you met her?"

Although he'd met dozens of people at the wedding and on subsequent visits, no image came to mind. "I don't think so."

"Well, it's about her little boy, Bobby. Something's happened."

Dylan's heart began to thud dully. Something told him he didn't want to know the rest, but he forced himself to ask anyway. "What about him?"

"He's disappeared. She thinks he's been kidnapped. Can you come, Dylan? Can you come right away?"

"Just tell me where," he said grimly, beckoning for paper and pencil. As soon as he had them, he jotted down the directions. "Have you talked to the police?"

"Justin's here now," she said, referring to her nephew who also happened to be the local sheriff. "He needs help, though. Kelsey wants this kept quiet. She won't let him call in the FBI or anyone else from outside."

The knee-jerk reaction of a panicked parent—or something more? "Why?" he asked.

"Let her explain. Just come. Please."

"I'm on my way."

"What?" Trish demanded, already standing as he reached for his jacket. "Why did Lizzy call you? What's happened?"

"It's about somebody named Kelsey. Her little boy's disappeared."

"Oh, no," Trish whispered, suddenly glancing at Laura as if to reassure herself that her daughter was right where she belonged. She regarded him worriedly. "Dylan, I don't know about this. Are you sure this is something you should get involved in? I know you're the best and I adore Kelsey and Bobby, but won't this be too hard?"

"I can't just turn my back," he said, wondering what the look Trish exchanged with Hardy was all about. "You obviously know this Kelsey person. Is there something more that I should know?"

"No," Trish insisted.

She said it without looking at him, which sure as anything meant she was covering up something. Trish had never been able to lie worth a hoot.

"Trish?"

"Just go."

He thought Hardy looked every bit as guilty as his sister, but he didn't have time to try to find out what they were hiding. If he didn't like the answers he got from Kelsey James, he'd come back here for the missing pieces.

"I'll try to call," he said, "but don't wait up for me."

"If you need people for a search, call me," Hardy said. "I can get all the men from White Pines to help out."

"Thanks. Let's see what's going on first."

If he had been anyplace other than Los Piños, Dylan would have called one of his buddies to take over right this second, because Trish was right—searching for missing kids tore him up inside. But there weren't a lot of private detectives nearby and time was critical in a situation like this. He had no choice. All he could do was pray that this disappearance would have a happy ending.

Kelsey felt as if someone had ripped out her heart. Anyone who'd been through med school and worked in an emergency room was used to terrible stress and was able to think clearly in a crisis. Despite all that training, though, she hadn't been able to form a coherent thought since the moment when she'd realized that Bobby was no longer playing in the backyard where she'd left him.

She had simply stood staring blankly at the open gate, frozen, until adrenaline kicked in. Then she had raced to the street, pounded frantically on doors, trailed by bewildered, helpful neighbors as she'd searched futilely for her son. Although plenty of people were outside on such a sunny summer day, no one had seen him leave the yard. No one had seen him toddling down the street. A child Bobby's age, alone, would have drawn attention.

She had no idea how long it had been—minutes, an hour—before she concluded that Bobby hadn't simply wandered away. By then both Justin and Lizzy had arrived, alerted by the neighbors. Justin had taken charge automatically, asking crisp, concise questions, organizing a search and leaving Lizzy to sit with her and try to keep her calm, when she wanted to be out searching herself.

With neighbors crowded around wanting to help, talking in hushed voices, Kelsey didn't feel calm, not after three cups of chamomile tea, not after the mild tranquilizer her friend had insisted she take. She wasn't sure she would ever be calm again, not until she had her baby back in her arms. This was her worst nightmare coming true. It didn't matter that no one had seen a stranger on the street. She knew what had happened. She knew who had taken Bobby. And why.

"It's Paul," she whispered finally, forcing herself to say aloud what had been tormenting her from the moment she'd realized Bobby was gone. "He's taken him. I know he has."

"You're probably right," Lizzy said, her tone soothing, as if she still feared that Kelsey would shatter at any second. "And I know you hate the man's guts, but isn't that better than a stranger? Paul won't hurt Bobby. Despite what a louse I think he is, I know he loved Bobby. He just wants money or drugs and Bobby's his bargaining chip. I think you can count on him being in touch. He's not going to run with him. He'll bring Bobby back the minute he gets what he wants."

"If he's desperate, who knows what he'll do?" Kelsey countered, shuddering.

This wasn't the old Paul, the one she'd fallen in love with. That Paul had been brilliant and driven and passionate. He had loved her in a way she'd never expected to be loved, charming her, convincing her in the end that he couldn't live without her, that they shouldn't wait till she finished med school or her residency to marry. It was ironic, really, that she'd struggled with the thought of marrying, just as Lizzy had, had finally rationalized that if Lizzy and Hank could juggle everything and make it work, so could she and Paul.

She couldn't exactly pinpoint when Paul had changed. Maybe he hadn't, not really. Maybe the drive she'd so admired in him at first had always been an obsessive need to win, to get what he wanted when he wanted it. He'd gotten her. He'd gotten the perfect job at the right brokerage house, then slaved to be the top broker, the quickest to earn a promotion. He'd convinced her to have a baby, even when she'd been so sure it was too soon, that their schedules were too demanding.

"We have the money. We can afford help," he'd

reasoned. "I want a family, while we're still young."

Now, always now. But she had gone along, because he had wanted it so much and she had wanted to please him. When Bobby came, every doubt she had had vanished. He was perfect. Paul was ecstatic and more driven than ever. Their son was going to have the best of everything.

"We have enough," she had told him more than once. But it was never enough for Paul, not for a kid whose family had struggled while he was growing up. He told her again and again that he knew the real meaning of adversity and he was determined that his wife and son would never catch so much as a glimpse of it. "Not as long as I'm able to bring in the big bucks just by putting in some long hours."

Then he had taken a nasty spill on a ski trip and fractured his wrist. It should have been little more than a minor inconvenience, but she knew now that that was when his addiction began. He'd taken the painkillers so he wouldn't have to slow down for so much as a second. He hadn't wanted to miss making a single commission. He'd never stopped.

She had cursed herself a thousand times for not realizing he was hooked. She was a doctor, for heaven's sake. She should have caught the signs, but she was too busy herself. In her own way, she was every bit as much of an overachiever as Paul.

Then there was a traffic accident. Paul's injuries were minor, the other driver's only slightly worse, but the routine bloodwork the police insisted on had revealed a high level of painkillers in his system. Confronted, he'd promised to stop taking them.

Shaken to the core, Kelsey had searched the house, found every last pill herself and flushed them all down the toilet. She had warned Paul to get help or lose her. She had wanted desperately to believe that he loved her and Bobby enough to quit.

A month later, she'd realized that her prescription pad was missing. Suspicious, she had made calls to half a dozen pharmacies, verified that her husband had gotten pills at every one of them and at who knew how many more. He had forged her signature on every prescription.

She had seen a lawyer that same day and had the divorce and custody papers drawn up. It was a drastic course of action, but she hadn't known what else to do. She had prayed that maybe the sight of the divorce papers would shock him into getting help. It hadn't. He'd simply taken more pills and blamed her for backing him into a corner.

She had known then that she couldn't let him ruin their lives, destroy her reputation. That night she had made a shaken and contrite Paul sign the papers. A week later, she'd moved to Texas, praying that he really would get the help he needed.

Now this. God help her, but she would kill him if he did anything to hurt her baby.

"We have to find him," she whispered.

"Which is why I called Dylan," Lizzy soothed. "He'll find him. Trish says he's the best private eye in Houston. Unlike Justin, he's probably handled cases like this a zillion times. He'll be fast and discreet."

"Where is he?" Kelsey whispered, her desperation mounting with every second that passed. Unless he'd spent it all on pills, Paul had plenty of money, enough to run to the ends of the earth. She might never find him or her baby.

"Shouldn't he be here by now?" she asked, edgy with impatience and ever-growing fear.

Lizzy glanced toward the doorway just then and smiled. "Here he is right now." She stood up, offering her seat opposite Kelsey at the kitchen table. "Dylan, this is Bobby's mom, Kelsey James. *Doctor* Kelsey James."

Kelsey felt her ice-cold hand being enveloped in a strong, reassuring grip. His size registered, too. He was a big man. Solid, with coal-black hair and a grim expression. She focused on his eyes, blue eyes that were clearly taking in everything. She had the feeling that his gaze missed nothing, that he could leave the room and describe every person, every item in it. At the same time there was a distance there, a cool detachment. Funny how she found that reassuring. He was a professional, she reminded herself, just what she needed. The best. He would find Bobby and bring him back. That was all that mattered.

"Tell me what happened," he suggested in a voice that was surprisingly gentle. He sounded almost as if he truly understood her pain. "Tell me exactly what you did, beginning with the moment you realized your boy was gone. Where was he? How long had he been out of your sight?"

"I've already told Justin everything," she said, not sure she could handle going over it again. It seemed surreal, as if she hadn't lived through it at all.

"Tell me," he said insistently. "I might catch something that Justin missed. Or you might remember something else. Every little detail is important."

He listened intently as Kelsey described everything that had happened, but when she mentioned Paul, something in his attentive expression changed. That disturbing coolness she'd noticed before subtly shifted into what she could only describe as icy disdain. He gazed at her with such piercing intensity that she shivered.

"You have full custody of your son?" he asked, as if it were some sort of crime.

She nodded, unsure why that seemed to unsettle him so.

"When was the last time the father saw him?" he asked, an inexplicable edge in his voice.

"Before we left Miami, about ten months ago. That was our agreement," she said, not explaining about the other part of that agreement, about her promise not to turn Paul in to the authorities. No one except Lizzy knew about that and no one ever would.

"You believe this was an abduction by a noncustodial parent," he said, summing up what she'd told him.

"I'm sure of it."

"Has he threatened to take Bobby before?"

"No, but—"

"Then why are you so certain?"

"I just am. It's the only thing that makes sense. Bobby wouldn't go off with a stranger, not without raising a fuss. Besides, I don't have enemies. I don't make a lot of money, so a demand for ransom's hardly likely. If someone wanted money in this town, they'd take an Adams.''

He nodded. He might be an outsider here, just as she was, but he obviously knew who had the power and the fortune.

''You haven't treated any kids who didn't make it, whose parents might blame you?'' he asked.

''No. Not since Miami.'' There had been a few inconsolable parents back then who'd wanted to cast blame on someone, *anyone,* and she'd been the easiest target. ''People who lose a child aren't always thinking clearly, but there were no malpractice suits. I doubt any of them would pursue me to Texas.''

''Okay, then, let's assume it's your ex. Have you got a picture of him? And I'll need one of Bobby, too. The most recent one you have.''

Relief flooded through her at his concrete suggestions. At last, something she could do. She went for the photo albums she kept in the living room, took out the most recent picture of Paul, then another of Bobby from his birthday party just a few weeks earlier. Ironically, the latest one she had of Paul had been taken on that ill-fated ski trip that had started his downward spiral.

''You're going to help?'' she asked as she handed the pictures to Dylan.

The question had been rhetorical, but for a moment she actually thought he might refuse. His expression was grim. He looked as if he wanted to say no. In fact, the word seemed to be on the tip of his tongue, but with Lizzy and others looking on expectantly, he finally sighed heavily.

''I'll help,'' he said at last.

After he'd gone, Kelsey kept telling herself that was a good thing, that she could count on this man, because Lizzy had said she could. But in her heart she kept wondering about that tiny hint of reluctance. It had something to do with her custody agreement with Paul. She was sure of it. Until she had mentioned that, Dylan Delacourt had been on her side. Now she couldn't help wondering if he was really on hers…or on Paul's.

Chapter Two

Dylan wasn't sure which had unsettled him more, gazing into Kelsey James's worried green eyes and feeling her fear, or discovering that she had sole custody of her son, that she had taken the boy away from his natural father. The former drew him to her, made him sympathetic. The latter made him want to withdraw from the case before he even got started.

He couldn't help making possibly faulty and unfair comparisons to his own situation. He instinctively lumped Kelsey in with Kit, assuming she too had backed a man into a desperate corner that had cost him his son. All of his own bitterness and resentment came surging back with a new focus: a slim, frightened mother who probably deserved better from him.

In the end, reason—and obligation to the

Adamses for their past kindnesses to his sister—won out. There was also the slim chance that Bobby could have been taken by someone other than his father. Until he knew for certain that Bobby was not in real danger, Dylan knew he had no choice. He had to take the case.

Of course, if he hadn't been persuaded by duty, there was the picture of Bobby, a robust little boy with an endearing grin. He couldn't help comparing him to Shane, wondering if his son was as healthy and happy as Bobby appeared to be in the picture. No matter what, Dylan knew he couldn't risk any harm coming to the child because his own personal demons kept him from pitching in to find him. With any luck they would locate Bobby quickly, Dylan's duty would be done, and he wouldn't have to spend much time around Kelsey James.

Eager to get away from her and to get started, he muttered an inane reassurance that neither of them believed, then left the crowded kitchen and went off in search of Justin Adams.

Justin might be a small-town sheriff, but he was smart and dedicated. He would have covered all the necessary bases and Dylan saw no need for them to duplicate efforts. Hopefully Justin would feel the same way, rather than going territorial on him the way a lot of cops did when faced with a private eye on their turf.

He found Justin outside by his patrol car, talking to his dispatcher over the radio. He signaled a greeting to Dylan.

"I want every last man on this, okay? Forget the shift roster and call them all in."

"Got it," the dispatcher said. "Want me to start calling motels? It could save time."

"Do it, Becky," Justin agreed. "Start with the immediate county, then widen it county by county. And make sure I can read your damn notes for once, okay?"

"There is nothing wrong with my handwriting," she responded tartly. "At least I *take* notes, unlike some people I could name."

Dylan would have smiled at the obviously familiar bickering if the circumstances had been different.

Justin sighed as he signed off. "The blasted woman's known me too long. She thinks she's the boss, even though I'm the one with the badge." He studied Dylan. "Lizzy called you, right? I figured she would."

"I hope you don't mind."

"Absolutely not. I can use all the manpower around on this, especially if you've got experience. Except for old Mr. Elliott, who wanders away from home and gets lost since his Alzheimer's has gotten worse, and the occasional missing dog, this is not something I'm used to handling. I'd be a whole lot more comfortable calling in the FBI, but Kelsey got so upset when I mentioned it, I backed off."

"Any idea what she's afraid of?"

Justin shook his head. "I'd be willing to bet Lizzy knows, though. One year as roommates in med school, and the two of them have been thick as thieves ever since. If we don't catch a break soon, I'll pound it out of her, if I have to. Figuratively, of course."

Sensing his frustration and sharing it, Dylan

grinned. "I'll help. Do you know anything about Paul James?"

"Only that Kelsey wanted to get away from him badly enough that she gave up a promising career in Miami to move here. It came up suddenly, despite Lizzy's pretense that they'd always talked about working together. One minute Lizzy was running the clinic by herself, the next Kelsey was here and living out at my grandfather's. Grandpa Harlan seemed real reluctant to let her and Bobby leave to move here in town, and I sensed it wasn't just because he'd grown attached to them. He had me check the security locks on this place top to bottom."

"Domestic violence?" Dylan speculated.

Justin shrugged. "Always a possibility, but my gut tells me no. A few years back when Patsy turned up here in town, she was running from an abusive husband. I don't see the same signs with Kelsey. She's at ease around men, for one thing."

"Patsy's your wife, right?" Dylan asked, trying to recall what he had heard about her situation. Just that she'd run from a husband who'd been a high-profile political candidate in another state, a man who had had a nasty temper. Bottom line, Justin would know better than most about how a victim of abuse would behave.

"Right. She had a little boy when we met and we have another one of our own now. She's at home with them, in a panic that something will happen to them if she turns her back for a second. Until we know for sure that Paul James is behind this, there will be a lot of other mothers who feel the same way. I'd like people to know as soon as we're sure that there's no need to lock the kids inside and bar their doors."

"Can't say I blame them, in the meantime," Dylan said. "How about I start running checks on Paul James? Maybe we can pick up a trail from credit-card receipts, see if he's in the area."

"Go for it," Justin agreed. "If you need access to a computer, use the one down at the station. I'll deputize you here and now to make it all nice and legal."

That was more than Dylan had hoped for. Normally, he preferred to operate on his own, but in this instance he was far from his own computer and other resources. A little hand-in-hand cooperation with the local authorities could cut through a lot of red tape. Having access to that computer would be a godsend. Besides, Justin struck him as a good man to work with. The past few minutes had established that he wasn't a hardliner with an attitude. He was the kind of sheriff Dylan admired, a man who just wanted to get the job done, utilizing whatever resources he could command.

"I'll let you know what I find out," he promised.

"I'm not worried about that," Justin told him. "Nothing gets past my dispatcher. Becky will be all over you while you're around. If you find so much as an itty-bitty clue, I'll know about it."

Dylan chuckled, liking the man more and more. "I should have known you weren't just trying to make my life easy."

Justin's expression sobered. "Nope. Just trying to

find that little boy before any harm comes to him.''

''Amen to that,'' Dylan said.

Unable to sit still a moment longer, Kelsey wandered into the living room and stared out the window at the two men talking on the sidewalk.

Over the last few months she had gotten to know Justin Adams. She trusted him, but she also knew that Bobby's disappearance was not the sort of thing he typically had to handle. She'd seen how upset he'd been by her refusal to call in the FBI. Maybe she was crazy, but she thought the fewer police involved, the better the chances of keeping Paul's secret and keeping Bobby safe. Watching Justin talk to Dylan, she could almost sense his relief at having someone with more expertise involved. She wished she was as confident.

She studied the private investigator, trying to overcome this fear that kept nagging at her. Once again, she was struck by his size. He was taller than Justin by a good three inches, putting him at six-three or so. He was broader through the shoulders as well. An ex-football hero, she was willing to bet. He moved with the ease of an athlete. None of that mattered, though. All she cared about was whether he could find her son.

She sensed Lizzy coming to stand beside her. Her friend hadn't strayed far from her side since this nightmare had begun. ''Looks like they're comparing notes,'' Kelsey said. ''They're probably wondering how I let something like this happen.''

''Don't be ridiculous. You didn't do anything wrong.''

"I should have watched him more closely. He shouldn't have been outside alone."

"He's a little boy, not a prisoner. He was in your own backyard. Maybe he wandered out front," Lizzy consoled her. "It only takes a second and if someone is watching, waiting for that to happen, there's not a thing you could do to prevent it."

"I should have—"

"Should-haves will make you crazy," Lizzy advised. "You're a wonderful mother. I won't listen to anyone—including you—who says otherwise."

Kelsey mustered a faint smile at Lizzy's fiercely protective tone.

"Why aren't they *doing* something?" she asked plaintively. "They're just standing around talking."

"Planning, coordinating," Lizzy corrected. "In the long run, it will save time."

Kelsey sighed, her gaze once again settling on the private investigator. "I don't think Dylan liked me much. He was so, I don't know, cold, I guess. At first I thought he was being professional, just trying to calm me down by seeming competent and practical, but now I'm not sure."

"Dylan liked you just fine," Lizzy reassured her. "I was there. He was just trying to get a fix on things."

Before Kelsey could debate her assessment, the phone rang, startling them both. Kelsey all but dived for it. "Hello," she shouted, then forced herself to quiet down. "Who is this?"

"Mommy?" a tentative little voice whispered.

Oh, sweet heaven, it was Bobby. She clutched the

phone so tightly her knuckles turned white. "Sweetie, is that you?"

"Hi, Mommy."

"Oh, baby," she whispered. Her knees went weak and she sank into a chair. She was dimly aware of Lizzy racing to the front door and shouting for Justin and Dylan. "Where are you, Bobby?"

"He's with me, of course," Paul said, interrupting.

Hearing his voice confirmed every one of her fears. He sounded as if he were on the edge. Too many pills? she wondered. Or not enough?

"Paul, please, bring him home. We'll forget this happened."

"Not just yet."

"Tell me what you want. I'll do anything. Just bring Bobby back. I know you didn't do this just because you missed him and wanted to spend time with him. If that had been the case, you'd have called."

"And begged? Is that what you want, Kelsey?"

"No," she said honestly. She wanted him to stay away, but he was back in her life for the moment, for better or for worse. "Paul, what is this about? What do you want?"

The only response was the quiet click of a receiver being put back into place. Kelsey stared at the silent phone in shock. He had hung up on her. She didn't know any more than she had before.

No, she told herself staunchly, that wasn't true. She knew for sure now that Paul had their son. She knew that Bobby was okay, at least for the moment.

For the moment. The phrase twisted and turned

in her thoughts, terrifying her. What about a moment from now? Or an hour? Then, to her chagrin, she burst into tears, gulping sobs erupting from deep inside. All the pent-up emotion of the past couple of hours came pouring out.

As if from a great distance, she could hear Lizzy murmuring to her. She was dimly aware of Justin barking orders into the phone. And then of a dip in the sofa as someone's weight settled next to her. For the second time that day, her hand was enveloped in Dylan Delacourt's. She recognized his touch, clung to him, because he was solid and reassuring and he was here.

"Talk to me," he commanded.

He tipped her chin up until she was forced to face him, forced to choke back another sob that threatened. He dug a clean handkerchief out of his pocket and silently handed it to her, then waited a minute until she was calmer.

"That was your ex?" he asked then.

She managed to nod. "Bobby first, then Paul."

"Good. Then we know what we're dealing with, who we're looking for. We know it wasn't a random act by a dangerous stranger, just a dad wanting to see his child."

She blinked back a fresh batch of tears. "That is good, isn't it?" she echoed, desperate for hope. Then she considered the rest of what he'd said, the faint note of sympathy in his voice. She didn't dare tell him he was wrong, that this wasn't about Paul's love for Bobby at all.

"The best news we've had all evening," he confirmed, giving her hand a squeeze. "We can narrow the search down from the get-go. It's a good sign, too, that he's willing to communicate with you, rather than simply disappearing with his son. We'll get a tap on the phone. Justin's already got an expert on the way. We can trace the next call, if you can keep him on the line.''

Kelsey recalled Paul's abrupt hangup. She sensed it had been more than an attempt to keep her from asking more questions, from demanding to speak with Bobby again. ''How long?'' she asked. ''I think he knows he can't stay on the line very long. That's probably why he hung up on me just now.''

''You'll do the best you can,'' Dylan told her. ''Sooner or later, he'll make a mistake.''

That's it? Kelsey wanted to shout. They were going to wait for Paul to make a mistake? Didn't they know that Paul didn't make mistakes? He was the champion of doing every last thing right.

Except for the pills, of course. She had caught him at that. She consoled herself with the memory. He was only human. He could slip up. She realized that Dylan was studying her intently with those deep blue eyes of his. They'd gone almost navy in the fading light and once more they were quietly assessing her, leaving her more shaken than she had been. She had a feeling he was doing it deliberately to unnerve her.

''What?'' he asked eventually. ''What aren't you telling us, Kelsey?''

''Nothing,'' she insisted, aware of the hint of defiance in her voice. ''I've told you everything.''

He shook his head. ''I don't believe you.''

She forced herself to meet his gaze, to not look away. "I can't help that."

"You want your son back, don't you?"

"Of course."

"Then you have to tell us the truth."

"I am, dammit."

"The whole truth," he added with emphasis.

"I am," she said again, but without the same vehemence.

Naturally Dylan didn't miss the difference. She could see it in his eyes. He knew she was lying.

What if she told him about the pills? She almost did, then caught herself. For if Paul found out she had broken her promise and told anyone, who knew what he would do? It wouldn't matter to him that he had broken their agreement first by coming after Bobby. No, she reassured herself again, she had to keep silent, for all their sakes.

Dylan wanted to shake the whole truth out of Kelsey James. She was obviously a bright woman. She had to know that forcing him and Justin to operate blindly just made everything twice as difficult as it needed to be.

The noise level in the living room climbed as neighbors discussed the call that had just come in. He saw Kelsey's gaze seek out Lizzy, probably for moral support, and realized he needed to get her alone, just the two of them. He had to find a way to gain her confidence, so that she would trust him with the whole truth.

"Let's go," he said.

"Where?" she demanded, balking.

He latched on to her hand and urged her back in the kitchen, then shooed everyone else out and shut the door. Kelsey looked as if she might protest, but then she sighed and sank onto a chair and accepted the cup of tea he handed her. She sipped automatically and stared warily at him over the rim of the cup, as if she sensed his displeasure. Dylan concluded that she was terrified enough without him coming down on her as hard as he wanted to. Tact wasn't his long suit, but maybe it was worth a try.

He turned a chair around and straddled it, took out a notebook and pen. "Okay, let's try this another way. Tell me about your ex."

She blinked rapidly, then studied her cup of tea as if it were the most important thing in her universe.

Dylan's short supply of patience was dwindling. "Kelsey, help me out here. I need to get a fix on this guy, get into his head."

"I know. It's just…" She shook her head. "I don't know where to start."

He bought her confusion. He sensed she really was struggling to sort through the information and put some order to it. He didn't need order. He needed raw facts. Still, he kept his tone mild as he suggested, "How about the beginning? Where did you meet? How long did you know him before you got married?"

She closed her eyes for a minute, as if the memories were painful. "He was a stockbroker," she began finally.

"Which firm?"

She named one of the biggest.

"Still there?"

"As far as I know."

He made a note, then nodded. "Go on."

"One of Paul's clients was a doctor at the hospital where I was in med school. We were just finishing rounds when he came in for an appointment to go over the man's portfolio. The doctor got called away on an emergency so he asked me to take Paul to the cafeteria and keep him company until he could get there." She regarded him wearily. "How is this helping? It's ancient history."

"Trust me. It will. So, was it love at first sight?" Dylan asked.

"Hardly," she said with a touch of wry humor. "I thought he was way too full of himself. A lot like you, in fact."

Dylan shrugged off the jibe. It wasn't the only thing he and Paul James had in common. He wondered how she would feel if she knew the truth about that.

"And?" he prodded.

"I never thought he would look twice at me."

"Why?" Dylan asked, genuinely incredulous at the suggestion that she wouldn't catch a man's attention.

"Let's just say I was a very bookish student. I didn't spend a lot of time with my appearance. He was very slick, very handsome, the ultimate yuppie. When I was studying, I was lucky to remember to put on lipstick and matching socks before I went out the door."

Dylan tried to reconcile the image she was painting with the woman seated across from him. He couldn't. Even in her shorts and T-shirt, her feet in sandals, she radiated both inner beauty and confidence. Her hair framed her face with the sort of tousled curls a man's fingers just itched to untangle. She had a scattering of freckles across her nose, but otherwise her complexion was near perfect. And those eyes—a man could sink in their glittering sea-green depths and go down for the third time happy. A sudden rush of heat told him he needed to avoid spending too much time gazing into those eyes.

"If you two were such a mismatch, how did you wind up together?"

"I don't know," she said with apparent bemusement. "Somehow we just clicked. Not overnight. It took a few weeks, but suddenly everything changed. Then things moved very quickly. We got married, moved into an old Coral Gables house that had great history and lousy plumbing and then Bobby came along. I was doing my residency in pediatrics by then."

"Sounds stressful. Was your husband a big help around the house?"

A smile tugged at the corners of her mouth. "Paul? You have to be kidding. The only thing he did was hire a nanny, then race off to the office. I don't know what you know about being a resident in a trauma center, but the hours are hell. Paul's were worse. Into the office before the market opened to get a jump on things, out with clients after Wall Street closed to celebrate the victories or solidify the relationship."

Dylan thought back to Kit's complaints about his work habits. More than once, she had accused him of being an absent husband and father. It sounded as if in the James marriage the two of them had shared the blame.

As if she sensed his disapproval, Kelsey said, "We did the best we could."

"Yeah, I'm sure you did," he said perfectly aware of the note of sarcasm that had crept into his voice.

Bright patches of color flamed in her cheeks. "You don't approve of me, do you, Mr. Dela-court?"

Dylan was surprised that she had called him on it. So the lady had a temper, after all. And good instincts. Maybe that could work to his advantage. He'd rather have her fighting mad than docile and defeated. He deliberately shrugged. "It's not my job to judge you," he said, careful to imply that he did just the same. "All I care about is finding Bobby."

After an instant's hesitation, she nodded. "Good. Then we can agree on that, at least."

He bit back his amusement at the tart tone. "You don't approve of me, either, do you, doctor?"

"Honestly?"

"Of course."

"I don't care what sort of foul-tempered beast you are. All I care about are results. You find my son and you will earn my undying devotion."

Dylan studied her thoughtfully. "Now there's a thought to make a man's heart go pitter-patter."

"Anything to motivate you," she retorted just as dryly.

For the first time in what had been a very grim

couple of hours, Dylan actually found something to laugh about.

"You and I are going to make a helluva team, doc."

Startled, she stared. "A team?"

He nodded. "From now on, you and I are going to stick together like glue."

It was the only way he could think of to be sure she didn't do something crazy to get her son back.

Chapter Three

Even as the words came out of his mouth, even as he mentally tried to justify them, Dylan cursed himself for the impulsive suggestion that he and Kelsey team up. Wasn't it enough that he was already operating cheek-by-jowl with a sheriff? Now he wanted to add an amateur into the mix. He was breaking every one of his long-standing, ironclad rules tonight.

Maybe it was because she'd purposely baited him, deliberately tried to establish boundaries. Hell, he liked boundaries. Loved them. And now he was pushing at them as if he couldn't wait to see them topple.

Oh, he recognized it for what it was. It was a male-female thing and this was definitely not a male-female situation. This was a job and he did not involve amateurs, especially clients, in his work. They lacked skill and objectivity, damned dangerous shortages. There went another hard-and-fast rule. Obviously, he'd lost it. He figured it had to be the eyes. He was a sucker for sad, sea-green eyes.

Truthfully, though, Kelsey didn't seem any more pleased by the idea than he was. In fact, she looked shocked.

"What do you want me to do?" she asked, regarding him with justifiable wariness.

He decided to back off in a hurry, just for the moment, not as if he were running scared, but just to establish a few of his own boundaries. There were things she could do to help…just not in the same place he was heading.

"Right now I'm going to the police station to run some checks. I want you to sit tight here. Make a list of questions to ask your ex when he calls. If he puts Bobby on the line, even for a second, ask what he's had to eat. Maybe he'll say something about a burger place we can trace or maybe he'll mention a specific diner. Ask what the room looks like or what he can see. Kids notice more than we give them credit for. And in case your husband is listening, try to make it sound as if you're just interested in hearing how Bobby's getting along. Know what I mean?"

Chin up, she nodded. "I think so. Post-preschool conversation, right? The sort of thing we'd talk about over milk and cookies?"

"Bingo. You catch on quick."

"Believe me, I am highly motivated." For an instant she looked lost again and very, very frightened. "I can't mess this up. I just can't."

Dylan tried to steel himself against the sympathy he was feeling. Still, he couldn't seem to prevent himself from giving her hand a reassuring squeeze. "You won't. You're doing fine, Kelsey."

She was, too. He was impressed with her despite himself. She was bright and tough. Love for her son, concern for him, radiated from her, but she hadn't allowed herself to give in to hysterics except for that one brief moment after her ex-husband's call. Nor was she giving in to Dylan's pressure to reveal whatever secret she was determined to keep. He didn't like it, but he had to admire her tenacity in clinging to whatever misguided principle she felt was so important.

He figured, though, that he'd gotten everything from her he could for the moment. He needed some distance to sort through what he'd learned, put it into perspective, and maybe get some cold, hard facts about Paul James from the computer at the sheriff's office.

"Want me to clear out some of these people before I go?" he asked.

She shook her head. "They just want to help. Lizzy will get them out later."

Another woman who could manage a small nation if she put her mind to it, he thought wryly. Lizzy had the Adams strength, as well as the family's fierce loyalty and protectiveness. He was definitely leaving Kelsey in good hands.

He ripped a piece of paper from his notebook and jotted down his beeper number. "If anything turns up, if you get another call, if you think of something, or if you just need to talk, call me."

She took the paper, holding it as tightly as if it were a lifeline. "Thank you."

"Get busy on those questions," he reminded her. "Be ready, in case he calls back."

"I will."

Dylan found himself fighting an odd reluctance to go. He knew there were better uses for his time, but he wanted to stay right here, offer whatever comfort he could. But Kelsey didn't need comfort from him. She needed his help in finding her son.

"I'll be in touch," he said and headed for the door, tucking his notebook into his back pocket as he went.

At the small but well-equipped sheriff's office, he was greeted by the dispatcher, who'd clearly been expecting him.

"Justin said you could use anything you need," Becky told him. "The computer's in his office. We've got several lines, so you won't be tying things up if you need to make calls. Don't worry about charges since you're making 'em as part of a case we're handling. You need anything, holler. There's coffee in here by me. It's strong and there's plenty of it."

"Thanks. I think I will have a cup. It could be a long night."

She poured it into a mug and handed it to him, then grinned. "Part of the service this time. After this, you're on your own." She winced as the radio screeched static. "Whoops! Got to go. I swear Billy Ray does that just to shoot my nerves to hell."

Dylan went into Justin's office and settled into the chair in front of the computer. He flipped through his notebook until he found the instructions Justin had given him for logging on. For the next few hours, he searched for any trace of Paul James, any mention of him no matter how insignificant. Credit information showed a man who paid his bills, mostly on time. He had no police record. There were no mentions of him in the Miami press.

He got on the phone and called a contact who could trace any credit-card activity. He woke the man out of a sound sleep, but by dawn he had a callback. Paul James wasn't using his credit cards, at least not so far. His last charge had been made a week ago, in Miami. He'd bought three new suits on sale at an upscale department store.

"Anything?" Justin asked, coming in and dropping wearily into the chair opposite Dylan. He looked as bad as Dylan felt.

Dylan shook his head. "Nothing. The credit-card trace was a bust, though I have to wonder why a man who planned on kidnapping his son would go out and buy three expensive new suits."

"Maybe he figured his next shopping trip would be a long time coming," Justin suggested.

"Or the sale was just too good to pass up," Dylan said lightly.

Justin's expression turned thoughtful. "Almost sounds like a man who doesn't intend to be gone all that long, doesn't it?"

"He can't be planning to take his son back to

Miami,'' Dylan protested. "He'd go straight to jail for violating the custody agreement.''

"Right. So, either he is just trying to scare Kelsey, or he wants something from her, or we're dealing with a nutcase who has no intention of taking his son anywhere except away from his mother.''

"To punish her,'' Dylan said, following Justin's logic with a sick feeling in his gut. "I hope to heaven you're wrong about that.''

"So do I,'' Justin said. "So do I.''

"Kelsey, you have to get some sleep,'' Lizzy said at dawn.

"I can't. As long as I don't know where Bobby is, I can't sleep. What if he calls again?''

"I'll wake you,'' Lizzy promised.

"No. I don't know how Paul will react if someone else answers the phone. He might hang up. He might get angry and hurt Bobby.''

"I just don't see him hurting Bobby,'' Lizzy countered. "That hasn't been his pattern, Kelsey. It's the one thing I don't think you need to worry about.''

"I can't help it. He sounded so edgy before. If he's been out of pills for a couple of days, he's probably in withdrawal. People do crazy things when they're coming down, things they otherwise might not do. Even the fact that he took Bobby in the first place is out of character. Paul never broke a law in his life until he got hooked on the painkillers. I never even saw him jaywalk. Heck, he'd dash two blocks just so his parking meter wouldn't run out. On the rare occasions when he got a parking ticket, he paid it the same day. Now he's violating a court order. That's the pills at work.''

Already jittery from nerves and lack of sleep, she jumped when the phone rang. She snatched it up. ''Bobby? Is that you?''

''Sorry,'' Dylan said. ''It's just me. I wanted to check in.''

''Oh,'' she said, sighing heavily.

''Anything happening over there?''

''Nothing.''

''Did you get any sleep?''

''Not a wink.''

''Kelsey, you're not going to do Bobby any good if you collapse. If you don't want to go to bed, at least nap on the sofa for a bit.''

''I can't,'' she said simply. ''Have you found anything?''

''Not yet, but I will,'' he said with reassuring confidence. ''You just hang tight. Is Lizzy still there?''

''Yes.''

''Let me talk to her a second, okay?''

Kelsey handed the phone to Lizzy, then listened openly to her end of the conversation. Lizzy's gaze settled on her and she nodded several times, murmuring agreement to whatever Dylan said. Kelsey figured she was the primary topic of conversation.

''I'll try,'' Lizzy promised before hanging up.

''I suppose you're to try to get me to get some sleep,'' Kelsey said.

''He has a point. I was saying the very same thing before he called.''

''I can't sleep,'' Kelsey protested.

''I could give you something.''

"Absolutely not," Kelsey said, horrified. After all, it was pills that had gotten them where they were now. The tranquilizer she had agreed to take the night before was one thing, but sleeping pills were another. Add in something to wake her back up again and she'd be on a roller-coaster. Who knew where it would end up? She could be in worse shape than her ex.

"You're not going to get hooked like Paul," Lizzy said, as if she'd read her mind.

"How do you know?"

"Because you don't have the same kind of obsessive personality he has." Lizzy clasped her shoulders and gazed into her eyes. "Sweetie, you need some sleep. If and when Paul does call again, you have to be thinking clearly. You can't be all strung out with exhaustion."

"And I can't be groggy with sleep, either."

Lizzy uttered a sigh of resignation. "Okay, at least go take a nice, warm bath."

Kelsey didn't want to leave the phone for a second, but she could see the sense in Lizzy's suggestion. A bath might relax some of the tension. And she would feel better in some fresh clothes, more in control.

"Okay," she agreed. "But I'll take the portable phone up with me."

Once she got upstairs, she considered taking a nice, invigorating cold shower instead, but the lure of a bath was more than she could pass up. She filled the tub with bubbles and sank into it up to her chin. The scent of lilacs, a distant memory from childhood summers in Maine, surrounded her. The water felt wonderful lapping gently against her skin. Her eyes drifted closed.

A soft tap on the bathroom door snapped her awake. Glancing down, she had just noticed that the bubbles were also a distant memory now, when the door inched open and Dylan poked his head in.

"You okay in here?" he asked, his gaze settling on her face for an instant, then drifting down.

Kelsey felt her nipples pucker under the intensity of his stare. A gentleman would have turned away, but he seemed to be frozen in place. There was enough heat in his gaze to warm the now-chilly bathwater. She couldn't seem to muster up the required indignation. Finally, he swallowed hard and backed out.

"I'll be out here when you're dressed," he said, his voice sounding choked.

As if her brain had finally clicked into gear, it registered that he wouldn't be there unless something had happened. Kelsey scrambled from the tub. Without bothering to dry herself, she pulled on a heavy terry-cloth robe and belted it as she flung open the door. Dylan was standing guard just outside, leaning against the wall.

"Why are you here? What's happened?" she demanded, standing toe-to-toe with him.

He put his hands on her shoulders. "Shh," he soothed. "It's okay. Nothing's happened. I just came over to relieve Lizzy for a bit. She said she'd sent you up to take a bath. When you didn't come back down, I thought I'd better check on you."

"Are you sure that's all?" she asked, still shaky.

"That's all. I swear it. If we find out something,

I'll tell you," he promised, his gaze locked with hers. "I won't hide anything."

"Even if it's bad?" she insisted.

He nodded. "Even if it's bad."

She believed him. There was something in his expression, something in the way he held her that made her believe that Dylan Delacourt would never lie to her. She had the feeling he was the kind of man who told the unvarnished truth, even when it was painful. She found that reassuring.

"Sorry I overreacted," she apologized.

"Sorry I intruded on your bath," he said, though the glimmer in his eyes suggested otherwise.

Disconcerted by the attraction that was totally inappropriate given the circumstances, Kelsey backed up a step. Dylan allowed his hands to fall away from her shoulders. She almost regretted that, but she faced him squarely.

"You look like hell," she observed. His cheeks were shadowed with the beginnings of a beard. He looked exhausted. "Give me a minute to get some clothes on and I'll fix breakfast. You can tell me what you did all night."

"Take your time. I'll cook," he said. "Have you got eggs and bacon? Scrambled okay?"

"Just toast for me."

"You need the protein," he said decisively and headed for the stairs.

Kelsey stared after him. She'd never had anyone around who showed the slightest inclination to take care of her. After all, she was a cool, competent doctor. Everyone knew she was the caregiver. Dylan apparently hadn't caught on to that yet. But he would, she thought with a sigh. For now, though, it was rather nice to take a few extra minutes dressing and know that when she got downstairs breakfast would be waiting.

Even if she wasn't hungry. Even if she had no intention of eating it.

Well, that was sweet, Delacourt, Dylan thought to himself as he marched back downstairs. Ogle the woman in her bath, why don't you? But he hadn't been able to tear his gaze away. Kelsey was an attractive woman and that baggy T-shirt and shorts he'd seen her wearing earlier had done nothing to enhance her natural beauty. Out of those, with all of her on display, so to speak, it was evident that she was a sensual, voluptuous woman. What man wouldn't look?

One who was concentrating on his job, he retorted mentally.

Kelsey James was a single mom whose boy was missing, not a potential pickup in some bar, he scolded himself as he went through her refrigerator, collecting eggs, bacon and butter. He found a pitcher of fresh orange juice and took that out, as well. By the time Kelsey joined him, he had breakfast on the table and his libido firmly in check.

That didn't mean he didn't cast a surreptitious gaze over her—just to make sure she was handling things okay, he assured himself. There were shadows under her eyes and her complexion was pale, but beyond that she appeared to be in control.

"Sorry about losing it for a minute upstairs," she said.

"Don't apologize. You're entitled to lose it every once in a while."

She glanced toward the phone, her expression forlorn. "Why doesn't he call back?"

"He will."

"The waiting is the worst. I'm used to being in charge, to being decisive. I make things better. I don't just sit around waiting."

"Always?" Dylan asked skeptically. "Aren't there times when even you can't control the rate at which a patient responds to treatment? Haven't you ever told a parent they just need to sit tight and wait?"

She frowned. "Okay, yes. I guess the difference is that I know how long it's likely to take for a medicine to kick in. I expect the delays. With this…" She shrugged, her expression helpless. "I don't know anything."

"What would you tell the parent of a sick child?"

"To be patient. To have faith. Pray."

"Don't you think maybe the same thing applies now?" he suggested.

Her expression brightened ever so slightly. "Yes. I suppose you're right. Patience and faith," she reiterated, as if he'd just given her a new mantra to recite. "Patience and faith."

She gazed at him then. "Thanks."

"Kelsey, let's establish a couple of ground rules. No more thanks. No more apologies. Deal?"

She nodded, started to say something, then cut herself off. "Sorry. Force of habit."

He grinned. "Caught yourself, huh? That's a start."

"How do you stand it?" she asked then.

Dylan wasn't sure what she was asking. "What?"

"Searching for a missing kid?"

He hesitated. He didn't want to lie to her, but for some reason he also didn't want her to lose confidence in him. Funny, when a few hours ago he would have given anything not to be involved in this case.

"I don't do it often," he said, choosing his words with care. "I usually prefer to turn this sort of case over to another private investigator."

"Why?"

"It's not my area of specialty, that's all."

She seemed shaken by that, just as he'd feared. "Then why did you agree to help?"

"Because I was here and it's best to get started immediately in a situation like this. There wasn't time to get another private eye in here." He leveled a look straight into her eyes, regretting the doubts that he had put there. "I won't let you down, Kelsey."

She kept her eyes locked with his, then nodded. "I know. Is that why you seemed so—I don't know—*reluctant* last night?"

So she had noticed that, had she? He'd have to remember that she was good at reading people. She probably had to do that a lot with kids who couldn't—or wouldn't—describe what was going on with them. He realized now that he wouldn't be able to hide anything from her.

Because he didn't want to get into the other reason for his reluctance, he took the easy way out and said, "Yes, that's exactly why." He rocked back in his chair. "But I'm in this now, Kelsey. We're going to find Bobby and bring him home."

"You sound so confident. I wish I felt that way."

"Patience and faith," he reminded her. "And a few of those prayers you like to recommend wouldn't be out of order, either."

Paul couldn't seem to sit still. He'd paced the motel room from one end to the other most of the night. That was the pills at work. They kept him on edge. If he'd been back in Miami, he'd have given up on sleep and gone back to the office, but he had Bobby with him now. He couldn't go running off and leave the boy all alone in a strange place.

He glanced over at the big double bed. Bobby looked lost in the middle of it. He was sprawled out, arms and legs going every which way, just the way he'd slept as a baby. To Paul's regret, there were still signs of tears staining his cheeks. The kid was confused and Paul couldn't blame him. He'd been all but snatched from his own backyard, hadn't been allowed to say goodbye to his mother.

There hadn't been any way around that, of course. Paul couldn't exactly walk into the house and announce that he'd come for his son. Kelsey would have driven him off with that high-and-mighty attitude she'd developed. He wasn't sure when she'd become such a stickler for the rules. If she'd been a little more flexible, things would never have turned out like this. She could have written a few prescriptions for him and he wouldn't have had to steal her prescription pads, then forge her signature to get what he needed. It wasn't as if he were some sort of streetwise drug addict. He was in real pain. His broken wrist had hurt like anything. Just because it had healed didn't mean the pain had gone away. Rainy days made it ache and in Miami, especially during spring and summer's tropical cloudbursts, there were plenty of those.

Besides, he had missed his son. He hadn't expected to, but he had. Bobby had looked up at him as if he were the greatest guy in the universe. He was probably the only person who'd ever looked at Paul that way. Not even Kelsey had thought he was infallible.

He'd gone to Texas on impulse. He'd planned on begging Kelsey for more pills. He'd figured she would balk at first, but eventually she would give them to him just to get rid of him.

Then he had seen his son and everything had changed. He'd wanted Bobby, too. He'd wanted to feel ten feet tall again.

It had been easy enough to get Bobby to come with him. The kid had been so excited by the prospect of going for ice cream with his daddy, he hadn't even hesitated. Only later, when he'd started missing his mom, had things gotten dicey. Bobby had cried so hard, Paul had finally relented and called the house, even though he figured Kelsey had probably brought in the police and accused him of kidnapping. It had been a risk, but he'd watched the second hand on his watch to be sure he didn't stay on the line long enough for the call to be traced.

Even that hadn't been enough for the kid. He'd wanted to go home. When Paul said no, Bobby had curled into a ball and eventually cried himself to sleep. Paul had felt about three inches tall, then, but it was too late to turn back. He needed those pills and he needed Bobby to get them.

Another day or two and Kelsey would be frantic enough that she'd give him anything he wanted.

Chapter Four

When Dylan left Kelsey in Lizzy's capable hands again at midmorning, he made a quick trip out to Trish's for a shower and a change of clothes. Laura's sunshine smile and eager greeting did as much to restore his spirits as the cool water and clean clothes.

"Unca Dyl, I swing?" she asked, trying to tug him toward the play area in the backyard. "Pweeze."

"Not now, angel. Uncle Dylan's got work to do." He scooped her up and planted a couple of noisy kisses on her cheeks until she giggled. Then he handed her to Trish, who was studying him with sisterly concern.

"Are you really okay?" she asked as she walked with him toward his car.

"Hanging in there."

"Dylan, everyone would understand if you wanted to back off. I'm sure we could get someone else in here."

"Sorry, kiddo. I always finish what I start." He skimmed a knuckle along Laura's cheek, even as he thought of a little boy over in Houston he prayed was safe at home. "You keep a close eye on this precious little girl of yours. I don't think I could bear it if anything happened to either of you. It's times like this that remind us what's really important in life."

"Nothing's going to happen to us, Dylan. And nothing is going to happen to Bobby. He's with his father."

"Wouldn't be the first time a kid was mistreated by a father," he pointed out. "Maybe that's why Kelsey left him, because he was abusing Bobby."

"Not Paul," Trish said with conviction. "Everyone says he was an okay guy, just not right for Kelsey."

He paused for a minute, intrigued by such a consensus of opinion from people who'd apparently never even met the guy. "Is that what everyone says? Who's everyone?"

Trish seemed surprised by the question. Her expression turned thoughtful. "Lizzy, I suppose," she said slowly. "Several others out at White Pines. When Kelsey came here, that was what we were all told, that her marriage hadn't worked out and she needed a change. No hint of anything other than a friendly divorce over irreconcilable differences."

Instinct kicked in and had Dylan wondering.

"Does that sound right to you? Lots of people get divorced and don't move halfway across the country, especially if they're established in a profession."

"And lots of people want to put plenty of distance between themselves and the past. There's nothing wrong with wanting a fresh start."

"Okay, yes," he agreed. Although he was instinctively sympathetic with Paul James and wanted badly to buy Trish's conclusion, he still couldn't shake the feeling that something wasn't right. "Think about this—Kelsey got full custody of her boy, not shared custody. Something had to be wrong for a court to do that, especially in this day and age, when a father's rights are taken into consideration more than they used to be."

Trish didn't look as if she'd been persuaded by his theory. "I suppose," she conceded halfheartedly. "Maybe it wasn't the court's decision, though."

"Meaning?"

"Maybe she and Paul worked it out between them. After all, they were both intelligent people. Maybe they just decided to keep the lawyers out of it and keep the hard feelings to a minimum. Then all the court had to do was sign off on their agreement, right?"

He nodded. "I suppose," he conceded as halfheartedly as she had a moment earlier. "It just doesn't feel right to me, though."

"Face it, Dylan. It would never feel right to you if the mother got sole custody. That's like waving a red flag in front of a bull. It'll get you going every time. Even though in the end it was your decision to give up custody of Shane, not Kit's, you blame her for it.''

"Okay, okay, I'm biased on the subject. I admit it.''

She regarded him curiously. "Have you told Kelsey about this particular bias?''

He shrugged off a nagging sense of guilt. "It hasn't come up.''

"Dylan, you're my brother and I love you. I think you're an incredible, skilled, caring investigator, but don't you think she has a right to know? She might conclude you don't have the objectivity to handle this case.''

"She probably would," he agreed. "Which is why I'm not telling her. I'm all she's got right now. She needs to believe I'm doing my best for her. She's shaky enough without adding a whole lot of doubts about me into the mix.''

Before his sister could respond to that, his beeper went off. He checked it, saw Kelsey's number and used his cell phone to call her back. Lizzy answered on the first ring.

"It's Dylan. What's up?''

"Paul called again.''

"Is Kelsey okay?''

"She's hanging in there.''

"I'll be right there.'' He gave Laura another peck on the cheek, then added one for his sister. "I'll check in when I can.''

"'Bye. Love you.''

"I love you, too.''

Checking his rearview mirror, he saw that Trish

stood watching him until his car curved into the pine forest that separated the house from the highway.

Maybe Trish was right. Maybe he should be telling Kelsey the whole story about Shane, letting her decide if she wanted him to stay on the job.

Not just yet, though. There was time enough for that after he found out what had happened when her ex-husband called. Maybe luck was finally on their side.

Kelsey was still shaking. She couldn't seem to stop. The trembling started inside, in the pit of her stomach. She had to get a grip. Falling apart wouldn't help anyone, least of all Bobby.

He was still okay. Paul had given her a whole thirty seconds to make sure of that. Bobby had barely said, "Hi, Mommy," when the phone was snatched away.

"Paul, please. I want to talk to him," she had begged.

"Another time."

Every one of the questions she had prepared so diligently at Dylan's direction flew right out of her head. She asked the first thing that popped into her mind. "Is he eating properly?"

"We're on vacation, Kelsey. He's getting all the junk food he wants." His tone was a mix of amused tolerance and familiar sarcasm.

Kelsey was about to protest, when she saw the absurdity of worrying about whether Bobby was getting enough carrots and broccoli.

"No argument? I'm amazed," Paul said. "You

were always such a stickler for the four basic food groups.''

She let that pass. ''What about clothes? Are you sure he's warm enough?''

''Kelsey, it's summer in Texas. He's plenty warm. If he needs clothes, I can afford to buy him some things.''

''Of course you can. That's not the point.'' Tears welled up and she batted at them impatiently. ''Paul, this is not a vacation and you know it. You've kidnapped him.''

''Now that is not a word I like to hear,'' he said, suddenly tense. ''You haven't called the police, have you?''

She hesitated, then saw no point in lying. Obviously he'd already guessed that she had. ''What else was I supposed to do when my son vanished from the backyard? Just let it pass and pray you were the one who had him?''

''He's *our* son, Kelsey. You might have custody, but he's still my boy, too.''

''Is that what this is about? Some belated sense of possessiveness?''

''We'll discuss it another time,'' he said tersely and hung up before she could think of some way to stop him.

''It wasn't long enough,'' she muttered, hearing the frantic note in her voice, the catch of a sob, and guessing that she was about to lose it again. She drew in a deep breath, fought for control, then met Lizzy's worried gaze. ''Call Dylan, will you? He needs to know about this. I need to get out of here for a second.''

She had gone outside and walked around the block, then circled it again at an even faster clip. She wasn't sure if she was running from something or just blocking out the pain. Either way, she was breathless by the time she got back home again and Dylan was waiting for her on the front lawn.

Seeing him there, his expression solemn, his gaze penetrating, she sighed with relief. She didn't know exactly what it was about him, but as long as she could see him, she had the feeling that everything would turn out okay. Was that something a good private investigator learned how to do, to reassure the victims of crimes, to instill confidence, to radiate a rock-solid strength? Or was it unique to this man?

"You okay?" he asked, his study of her face never wavering.

"Just peachy," she responded acerbically.

"Okay, dumb question. Let's get to the point," he said briskly. "Tell me what Paul said when he called."

His quick reversion to strict professionalism calmed her. But then she thought back to the brief conversation and felt tears of frustration build again. "Nothing, dammit. I forgot all the questions I had planned, but he was so careful. He wouldn't give me so much as a hint about where they are. He barely let Bobby say hello."

"Did Bobby sound okay?"

Thinking of that sweet whisper of a greeting, she choked up and settled for nodding.

Dylan tucked a finger under her chin and forced her gaze up. "He didn't sound frightened, did he?"

She thought about it. He'd only said a word or

two, so it was hard to tell, but no, he hadn't sounded scared. "Actually, no," she admitted.

He smiled. "See? He's doing okay. He probably thinks this is just a big adventure with his dad. It's the grown-ups back here who are scared, not your son."

"That's good, isn't it?" she said, clinging to it. As furious as she was with Paul, this could be so much worse. Bobby was fine. He just wasn't where he belonged—with her.

She met Dylan's gaze. "Thank you for making me see that. I won't stop worrying until he's back here, but I'm not as panicked as I was."

Dylan nodded, then glanced toward the house where neighbors were still gathered in small groups on the lawn and on the porch. "Feel like another walk around the block?"

"Why?"

"Fewer people. There are a few more questions I need to ask you."

"I've already told you everything," she protested. "Paul was only on the line a minute."

Dylan grinned. "You just think you've told me everything." He gestured toward the sidewalk. "You game?"

Uncertain what more she could possibly add, she still set off around the block again, albeit at a slower pace. Suddenly she was aware of just how hot it was. The late morning heat rose from the cement in waves. The sun beat down, making her clothes cling and her hair damp. It was hardly the time for a stroll, but then this wasn't about getting a little exercise or even settling her nerves. It was about Dylan grilling her, she realized as he began to bombard her with questions.

"First thing you heard when you picked up the phone?" he asked.

"Bobby's voice," she said at once.

"Right away? There wasn't a pause. Kids don't usually speak right off. It takes them a second to realize there's somebody on the line."

She thought back. Had she heard Paul coaching him? Telling him to say hi to mommy? "Paul," she said with a sense of amazement. "I heard him telling Bobby to say something."

Dylan nodded his approval. "Good. Anything else? Cars? Dishes being set down on a counter? Music? A clock striking the hour? A church bell?"

Kelsey slowed her pace, then stopped and closed her eyes, listening to the silence, listening with everything in her for some clue. Finally she sighed with frustration. "Nothing," she said, staring at Dylan in disappointment.

"No TV in the background?"

"No. I told you, I didn't hear anything except Bobby's voice, then Paul's."

"What about road noise? Could he have been on a cell phone?"

"He has a cell phone. No broker can live without one. They might miss the big deal," she said sarcastically. "But it didn't sound like that. It was just…" She shrugged. "I'm sorry. It was just a regular call from some everyday phone. They could have been anywhere."

He turned her to face him, kept his hands on her shoulders. "It's okay. You'll listen differently next time. Pay less attention to what's said and more to the background.''

''But you told me to ask questions,'' she retorted with mounting frustration. ''How can I ask questions and listen to the background all at once? God, I can't do this. I'm no good at it.''

''You're not supposed to be good at it. No one should ever have to be good at it,'' Dylan said heatedly. ''But you'll do the best you can.''

She gazed up at him, feeling that unfamiliar wave of helplessness roll over her again. ''I hate this,'' she said vehemently. ''I'm his mother. I should have been able to protect him. I'm a doctor. I make other people's kids well and I can't even keep my own safe.''

''You're a doctor and a mother, not God,'' Dylan reminded her with surprising gentleness. ''Nobody expects perfection.''

''I do,'' she said. ''My whole life has been about getting it right. My parents were overachievers, who expected me to excel, and I did. Full scholarship to the University of Miami med school. Straight A's. Top of my class. I had my pick of internships and residencies. Kelsey Donnelly James was one of the best and brightest,'' she said with self-derision. ''What does it matter when my son is snatched right out from under my nose?''

Dylan's grasp of her shoulders tightened just enough to snap her out of her bout with self-pity. ''Did you teach him not to go anywhere with strangers?''

''Of course.''

"So if some stranger had come up to him in your backyard, what would he have done?"

"Screamed for me. Run to the house. That's what I always told him, make a lot of noise and never, ever go with somebody he didn't know."

"Right. So you prepared him for that threat."

She nodded, beginning to see his point.

"You didn't think you needed to tell him not to go with his own father, did you?"

"No," she conceded, exhaling a tiny sigh. But she should have. Wasn't Paul the bigger threat, maybe not more dangerous than a stranger, but certainly the most likely candidate to come after Bobby? In the back of her mind wasn't that precisely why she had insisted on sole custody, why she had moved so far from Miami? She said none of that to Dylan.

"Bobby had no idea that going with his dad was wrong," Dylan consoled her. "This is about Paul violating a court order, not anything you did or didn't do to protect your son."

"Still, if I'd been watching more closely, Paul couldn't have gotten to him."

"You plan on never working at the clinic again?"

She regarded him indignantly. "Of course not."

"You going to take Bobby inside and lock the doors and windows until he's old enough for college?"

"No," she said, even though the idea was so preposterous that it didn't even deserve a response.

"Kelsey, there are risks, especially in the world we live in today. Los Piños is a great little community. It probably has fewer crimes than most places. You can prevent a lot of bad things, you can prepare for some, but just when you think you have every angle covered, something unexpected can come along. Unless you want to stop living, you can't protect Bobby from every single one of them.'' His gaze locked on hers and he spoke with added emphasis. ''You did not do anything wrong. I can't say that strongly enough.''

She wanted to believe that, almost did because Dylan said it so forcefully, but until her dying day she knew there would always be a nagging doubt that she could have done something more.

What, though? Would she really have warned Bobby about his dad, turned a little boy against his own father? Would she have gone that far? A more vindictive woman certainly would have, maybe even one with a stronger sense of self-preservation. She'd believed the court-approved custody agreement and distance were enough. Paul had desperately wanted her silence, because anything else would have destroyed his career. He'd wanted that agreement as badly as she had. So she'd trusted him to honor it.

And for reasons that definitely escaped her now, she hadn't wanted to take away Bobby's good memories of his dad. She'd wanted those to be salvaged for some future date when Paul got his act together and could be trusted to be with his son again.

''It doesn't matter now,'' she said wearily. ''He's gone. I just have to concentrate on getting him back.''

''Exactly. Let's stay focused on that.'' He studied her intently. ''Just a couple more questions about the call, okay?''

She started to protest that it was a waste of time, then stopped. "Fine. Anything."

"What was the first thing you asked Paul?"

"About what Bobby was eating. He said junk food."

Dylan nodded. "Nothing specific, though?"

"No, just junk food."

"And then?"

"About his clothes. If he was warm enough."

"And what did he tell you?"

"That it was summer in Texas," she repeated, then stopped as she realized what she'd said. "He said Texas." She felt a grin starting to spread across her face. "They're still in Texas." It was such a small clue, but she felt like jumping up and down.

Dylan grinned back. "See? I told you there was more locked away in your memory than you realized. That's a start. We don't have the whole country to worry about right now, just the state. He's sticking close, Kelsey. I can feel it. And if he's nearby, we'll find him." His gaze settled on her. "Will you be all right? I want to get back to work."

She nodded. "I'll be fine. Where are you going? What will you do now?"

"I'll stop by the sheriff's office. I want to touch base with Justin, see if they've come up with anything. I've got some calls out for information. I need to check to see what's turned up." He glanced toward the house. "Lizzy waiting inside?"

Kelsey nodded. "Yes. I don't know what I'd do without her, but she can't stay forever. Somebody needs to be at the clinic. We have patients scheduled." She thought of a whole slew of kids who were due in this week for their preschool checkups, all her responsibility. "I should—"

Dylan cut her off. "You should be right here. Everything else can wait. I'm sure if someone needs a doctor for an emergency, they'll know to reach Lizzy here. She can have the clinic's calls forwarded."

"But there are shots," she protested. "The kids need them for school."

"And they'll get them. We'll have Bobby home soon and you'll get right back to work. A few days won't make that much difference."

She supposed he was right, but it just seemed so irresponsible to be putting her own crisis ahead of duty. Her uptight mother would be appalled. A Donnelly always took care of obligations, no matter what. How many times had she heard that? How many disappointments had she endured as a child because duty called, keeping one or both of her parents away from some triumph that mattered to Kelsey, but no one else, at least not enough for them to be there? She halted that line of thinking, because it was counterproductive. It was in the past. Everyone had history they'd had to overcome. Her life was no different.

In the here and now, she could admit that a few delayed shots wouldn't be the end of the world. The kids would no doubt relish the reprieve and the parents would understand. So would the school system, if it came to that. This was a town where people mattered more than schedules and rules. And if some poor bureaucrat didn't believe that, Harlan Adams would be more than willing to explain it to him.

"I'll bet we could search the whole town and not find a single kid who's upset at not getting a shot," Dylan teased gently, as if he'd read her mind.

"You're probably right about that, though the word is that I am very slick with a needle. In and out before they even know what hit them. And I have some very good lollipops for the brave."

He looked taken aback by her evident pride in that particular skill. "I'll keep that in mind next time I decide to get a flu shot," he said. "Probably won't be any time this century, though, so don't keep an appointment open for me."

She laughed at the thought of this tough guy being scared of shots. "Why Dylan Delacourt, don't tell me you're afraid of needles."

"Afraid?" he retorted indignantly. "No way. Just of the people who go poking around with them and especially of those who so obviously enjoy it." He gave her a disconcerting once-over. "Though I'll bet if anyone could give me a shot and make me like it, it would be you, doc."

With that and a wink, he was gone before she could fully absorb the compliment. What was wrong with her? Her son was missing and she was getting all warm and mushy inside because a private investigator was acting mildly flirtatious. He probably hadn't even meant anything by it. He'd just been trying to lighten the mood, to lift up her spirits.

And it had worked, too. She went back inside feeling a whole lot better than she had when she'd hung up after Paul's last call.

"Is that pink in your cheeks from the sun or from

a certain detective?'' Lizzy demanded when Kelsey found her in the kitchen.

"It's hot out,'' Kelsey declared, but she kept her gaze averted because Lizzy had always been able to see right through her.

"Whatever it is,'' Lizzy replied, "it's good to see some color back in your face. You've been too pale. I've been worried. You were starting to look defeated. Now you look as if your fighting spirit is coming back.''

"Oh, yes,'' Kelsey declared. "If I ever get close enough to Paul to get my hands around his neck, he's a dead man.''

Lizzy beamed. "Now there's a thought.'' She held out a glass of iced tea. "Shall we toast to it?''

Kelsey took the tea, rubbed the icy glass against her cheek, then took a long swallow, savoring it as it soothed her parched throat. She felt better than she had in more than twenty-four hours. Her emotions were no longer on such a wild roller-coaster. She knew now exactly what she was dealing with. Paul had Bobby somewhere in Texas. It was a big state, but not impossible to search, not with the people and resources committed to helping her.

There was comfort in that, she realized. Dylan had made the illusion of control possible by putting everything into clear focus, by giving her concrete things to do when Paul called, by ferreting out the one clue that had slipped past her. She would be listening even closer next time. Not so much as a whisper of background noise would escape her. If getting Bobby back depended on it, she would listen like a hawk.

And with Dylan's help, she would sort through the most innocuous of clues until she had her precious son back home.

Chapter Five

Dylan had never been so thoroughly frustrated in his entire career. They couldn't seem to catch a break. Paul James wasn't making mistakes. He wasn't leaving a trail. Even Kelsey's discovery that he was apparently holding Bobby someplace in Texas wasn't going anywhere.

And with every hour that passed, there was a very real likelihood that he would slip out of their grasp for good, if that was his intention. He was that clever.

"Damn," Dylan muttered, looking over the list Becky had compiled of the motels within a hundred-mile radius. "Not a sign of him. I was so sure he was close by."

"I've moved on to the next counties," the dispatcher told him, her own frustration evident.

''Where can he be staying? Surely he wouldn't take that boy to some cheap, fleabag place. Do you think he's left the area? If he's gone to Dallas or Fort Worth or any other big city, there are too many hotels and motels for me to check between handling other calls. We'd have to have more help.''

Dylan didn't even want to consider that just yet, but it was a real possibility he couldn't ignore. A father traveling with his son wouldn't stand out in a metropolitan area the way he would in some small town where people were attuned to the comings and goings of strangers.

Worse, despite what he'd said to Kelsey in this morning's call, by now Paul could have left Texas entirely. He could have hopped a plane and fled the country, for that matter. That's what Dylan would have done, if he'd gotten a notion to take Shane. He would have gone as far away from Texas as he possibly could to stay out of the law's reach.

Of course, as far as he knew, the two situations were entirely different. He'd voluntarily given up custody of Shane for his son's own good. He'd made a solemn vow—not just to Kit, but to himself—that he wouldn't intrude in the boy's life again.

For the most part, he'd stuck to that promise. Except for one person, no one knew about the lapses and he prayed to God no one else ever would.

He'd made three trips to see Shane, only from a distance, of course. Just to reassure himself that the boy was getting along okay. He believed with all his heart that he'd done the right thing in giving up custody, but he'd needed to see the evidence of it with his own eyes.

It hadn't been hard to track Kit and her new husband down. They were living in a fancy suburb of Houston on the opposite side of town from Dylan's own place. It wasn't like they'd made a secret of it. He hadn't had to go digging through confidential records to find them. They were in the phone book for anyone to find. That was how much Kit had trusted him to keep his word.

And he had—more or less. He'd just driven through the neighborhood a couple of times during the first few months after she'd remarried. Okay, once he'd lingered down the block from the house, waited until he'd seen Shane playing in the yard with his new brothers.

Even now his throat tightened as he recalled how happy the boy had seemed. Shane had dogged the footsteps of his new big brothers, trying to keep up with them, and they had been oh-so-patient with a toddler tagging after them. Watching them with a mix of amusement, nostalgia and sorrow, he knew he hadn't been half that patient with his own kid brothers. In the end, he had driven away reassured.

It had been over a year before he'd paid another visit. He'd realized one day in October that Shane would probably be in preschool. The fact that he'd missed his boy's first day of school had overwhelmed him. Another cursory check of the phone book had led him to the school closest to Kit's. He'd parked a block away from the playground, then kept his eyes peeled for some sign of his dark-haired son.

He'd spotted Kit first, waiting on the sidewalk as Shane ran out, a red lunch box in one hand and a brightly colored finger painting in the other. He'd been chattering a mile a minute even before he reached his mother. Dylan had longed to hear the sound of his voice, but he'd been too far away. Thankfully, Kit hadn't seen him…or so he'd thought at the time.

A week later the finger painting had turned up in his mail. The picture had been a childish rendering of a mother, a father and three boys. Even though no note had been attached, the message was unmistakable—this was Shane's family now.

That picture and a few photos that he'd taken from Shane's baby album were all he had of his son. He kept them tucked away in a dresser drawer, so no one else would know that he hadn't completely forgotten the little boy he'd given up.

He needed his family to believe he was okay with his decision, that he never looked back. He couldn't take having to defend the choice over and over again. Though his father and brothers avoided the topic, it was always there, albeit unspoken, especially around holidays.

Only Trish and his mother dared to broach the subject aloud—Trish out of love and concern, his mother for her own selfish reasons. In fact, his mother never let up with her pestering. She had complained bitterly about giving up all rights to see her first grandchild, at least until Trish had had Laura. Now the grumbling had died down, but there were still enough barbs directed his way that Dylan knew she hadn't entirely forgiven him. He suspected his father also resented his decision to give up the first male heir to the Delacourt oil dynasty, but after Dylan's rebellious defection from the family business, Bryce Delacourt had learned his lesson. He knew better than to bring it up.

So they all lived with Dylan's decision in relative silence. Dylan couldn't help wondering if Paul James had made the same kind of commitment to Kelsey for all the right reasons, then spent months of hell second-guessing himself before finally breaking and following her to Texas. Dylan wanted to believe he was a better man because he'd never put Kit through the kind of pain Kelsey was enduring now, but who knew how close he'd come to breaking his vow without realizing it? Those surreptitious visits had certainly crossed the line, albeit not as dramatically as what Paul had done.

Then came another nagging doubt. What if Kelsey deserved what was happening? What if he'd completely misread the kind of person she was? What if she had forced Paul into relinquishing custody? Had she been holding something over his head? Was that the secret she was guarding so tenaciously? Maybe she'd even blackmailed him into giving up his son.

Sweet heaven, he was losing it. He'd been around Kelsey enough in the past forty-eight hours to know better. That wasn't the kind of woman she was. His gut instincts about people were rarely wrong. He hadn't even been wrong about Kit. She was a good woman, just all wrong for marriage to a man like him. As much as he'd wanted to blame her, even hate her, for the way things had turned out, he'd known the fault for their failed marriage was as much his as hers. Reason just wasn't always enough to counteract bitterness.

He glanced up and realized he'd been staring blankly at Becky's report for some time. The dispatcher was regarding him with blatant curiosity.

"You okay?" she asked.

"I'd be a whole lot better if we could pick up a trail. Where's Justin? Has he called in?"

"Right before you got here. He'll be back in five minutes. He wants you to wait."

"I'm not going anywhere," Dylan said and poured himself another cup of coffee before sitting down to go over Becky's list of motels one more time.

Justin came in moments later, looking frazzled and frustrated. "Nothing," he muttered with disgust. "I've had men questioning everybody in the whole town and nobody saw anything yesterday. I've checked the flights from Miami coming into Dallas-Fort Worth yesterday. If Paul James was on one of them, he was using a pseudonym and paid cash. The rental-car people weren't any help, either. He would have had to use his driver's license to get a car and he didn't."

"Phony papers?" Dylan suggested.

"Or he drove from Miami."

"On the off chance you're right, let's call the DMV in Florida and get his car registration," Dylan said. "It'll give us something to look for. I have a man in Tallahassee I've used before. I can call him. Then we can get Miami P.D. to take a look around Paul's place there to see if the car's still in the vicinity. You call the police and make the request official."

Justin nodded, his expression brightening. "I'd

give just about anything for an honest-to-God lead about now. Lizzy says Kelsey's holding up okay, but the longer this drags on the more likely I'm going to have Grandpa Harlan down here busting my chops for not getting it resolved. Believe me, I do not need my grandfather getting a notion in his head to play cop.''

Dylan grinned. He could totally understand Justin's concern. A powerful, strong-willed man like Harlan Adams, who wasn't used to sitting on the sidelines and waiting, could make a policeman's or a private investigator's life miserable. It would be worse if they were related.

''Then let's make those calls,'' Dylan said, already reaching for the phone. While he waited for his contact to call back, he and Justin went over Becky's list one more time to see if there was anything about any of the hotels and the guests they'd acknowledged that bore further checking.

A few minutes later, Dylan's man in Tallahassee called back with the car description and tag number. Dylan passed the information to Justin, who called Miami police and requested assistance.

Dylan paced while they awaited a return call. It took a whole helluva lot longer than he would have liked, but when the news came back, it was good. There was no sign of Paul James's car at his home or in the lot by his office. The police promised to check the airport lots within the next few hours and get back to them about that.

''For now we can work on the assumption that he drove that car here,'' Justin said triumphantly, then bellowed, ''Becky!''

"I'm right here, not in the next county," she retorted from just outside the door.

"Call those hotels back and check to see if this tag number is on any car in their lots." He added a description of the car, as well. "For all we know he could have put stolen plates on it by now."

"Or stopped off and registered it in another state, if he's planning on settling someplace new with Bobby," Dylan said thoughtfully. "Damn. Have you called his employer in Miami?"

Justin nodded. "First thing this morning after we knew for sure he had Bobby. As far as his boss knew, Paul is just on a two-week vacation."

Dylan couldn't hide his surprise. "What did you make of that?"

"Either he was covering his tracks or he fully intends to return home in a couple of weeks."

"He can't go back with Bobby," Dylan protested. "Does that mean he intends to give him back to Kelsey before he goes home?" He shoved away from the desk and started to pace again. "Is this some sort of temporary game with him?"

"I'd give anything to be able to get inside this guy's head," Justin said. "I can't figure out if he's got a screw loose, if he's desperate, or if he's just plain mean."

"Or if he's just a dad who misses his son," Dylan said quietly.

Justin's gaze narrowed. "You sound sympathetic. Whose side are you on here?"

"Kelsey's, of course," he said, but he couldn't hide the defensive note in his voice.

"You sure of that? Because if you're not, I'll see

to it you're off the case and out of town before you know it.''

"Look, I'll admit to having a custody issue of my own, but it's not influencing how I handle this case. I'm on Kelsey's side.''

"I sure as hell hope so,'' Justin said, his tone and his steady gaze a warning.

"If that changes, you'll be the second to know,'' Dylan promised. "The first person I'll tell is Kelsey.''

People kept coming and going. It was driving Kelsey just a little bit crazy. They all meant well. They all wanted to help, some by offering to join the search, some by bringing food for all the other people dropping by, some just by expressing their concern.

The one person she wanted to see, Dylan, hadn't been by in hours. Nor had he called with any news. Lizzy had kept her from calling him by reminding her that he and Justin were doing their jobs.

"Leave them alone and let them work,'' Lizzy said. "Now I am going to shoo everybody out of here and you're going to get some rest.''

Before Kelsey could protest, Lizzy pointed her toward the stairs. "There's a phone by the bed. If it rings, you'll be able to grab it. If you can't sleep, fine. At least close your eyes and rest. Otherwise, you're going to collapse. The clinic's going to be a madhouse when we open it again. I can't afford to have the pediatrician out sick.''

Kelsey had finally started toward the stairs, but her head snapped back. "You closed the clinic?''

"Who was going to treat anybody? You and I are both here. People will just go to Garden City if there's an emergency. That's what they did before the clinic opened. Besides, I'm pretty sure my father has forbidden anyone to have a medical emergency while we're in the midst of this crisis. You know how people around here listen to Harlan Adams."

Kelsey chuckled. He very well might have. He would have been affronted if anyone dared to defy him, too. When her chuckle threatened to turn into hysteria, she knew Lizzy was right. She needed sleep.

Still, she went upstairs reluctantly. One of the reasons she'd avoided going to her room was because to get there she had to pass Bobby's. She hadn't been sure she could bear to walk by it, knowing it was empty, that he might never see it again. Now, she dragged in a deep breath and paused in the doorway.

The room was exactly the way it had been when he'd disappeared, a mess. She smiled at the clutter, something she didn't always do. She had bought a huge old trunk at a garage sale and painted it bright colors. It was meant to be a toy chest, but as far as she could tell nothing was in it.

Bobby's favorite toys—and he had almost none that weren't favorites to hear him tell it—were all over the floor, scattered under the bed, and piled on the colorful desk that had been one of his birthday gifts from Harlan Adams. Stuffed animals Bobby claimed to be getting too big for still seemed to find their way onto his bed. She went in and picked up his Pooh bear.

Well-worn from all the loving a little boy could give it, Pooh smelled of grass stains and orange juice and Bobby. The mixture of scents brought tears to her eyes and she sank down on the edge of the bed feeling lost. Had Bobby been able to sleep without his beloved bear? Had he asked for it? How had Paul consoled him? By buying him a replacement? Or just ordering him to be a big boy and forget Pooh? That sounded more like Paul.

Suddenly she was sobbing, hot, scalding tears of fury and betrayal this time. Clutching the fragile bear, she rocked back and forth, letting her tears roll down her cheeks until they soaked her blouse and eventually Pooh himself. He'd seen his share of tears before, she knew, and her own mixed with Bobby's.

"Hey, hey, what's this?"

She didn't have to look up to know it was Dylan. His voice was becoming as familiar to her as her son's. She felt the bed sink under his weight and the next thing she knew he had gathered her close, Pooh smushed between them. His murmured words of comfort were mostly nonsensical, but it was the sound of his voice that soothed, the strength of his embrace that gave comfort. She gave herself over to it, letting the tears flow.

"Oh, God, Dylan, what if I never see him again?" she whispered, her voice muffled against his chest.

"You will," he vowed.

She blinked back tears and drew back to gaze at him. "You sound so sure. Has something happened?"

"We found out Paul's car isn't at his house or his office. Justin and I agree it could mean he drove here. We also found out he's only taken a two-week vacation at work. He hasn't quit."

Kelsey stared at him mutely, trying to grasp the implications.

"Kelsey, did you hear what I said?"

She nodded. "I just don't know what it means."

"It means we not only have Bobby and Paul to look for, but a specific car. We have police all over the state checking hotel and motel parking lots and registration books. We also think it could mean that Paul doesn't intend to go on the run with Bobby, maybe not even to keep him."

She felt the tight knot in her stomach ease ever so slightly. "He'll bring him back, then," she said, half to herself. Hadn't she believed from the beginning that Paul had only done this to frighten her, to back her into a corner so she would help him get more pills? It all fit. She just had to wait him out, wait for his demand.

And then what? Would she give him a supply of narcotics? How could she do that in good conscience? And if she did it this time, would he simply come back again and again, using Bobby for leverage each time? No, she had to put a stop to it now, but how?

She looked at Dylan, noted how intently he was watching her, and realized just how certain he already was that there was more to this than she had told him. Could she tell him the rest? Did she dare? Would he help her keep the secret or feel compelled to turn Paul in to the authorities?

She was struck by a sudden thought. Paul was already in trouble with the police. He'd violated a court order when he took Bobby. That alone should be enough to put him in jail and keep him from coming after her for more pills. All they had to do was catch him and her problems would be over, for however long such a sentence lasted. Maybe jail would be the best for him. He'd have to get over his addiction in there. Still, the thought of Paul in jail sent a chill down her spine.

"Kelsey?"

She glanced at Dylan. "What?"

"What is going on in that head of yours? I can practically see the wheels turning."

"I was just thinking about the future," she said, which was honest as far as it went.

"Oh?"

"Will Paul go to jail?"

"Most likely."

"For how long?"

Dylan shook his head. "I'm not certain. If he brings Bobby back on his own, it would probably help."

"What if I didn't press charges?"

Dylan stared at her, clearly shocked. "Why the hell would you not press charges?"

"Because…" She searched for an explanation that made sense. She wasn't sure there was one. Paul had to pay. She knew that, but the thought of Bobby's dad being in jail made her physically ill. What would Bobby think when he grew up and realized his mother was responsible for putting his father in prison? "I guess I'm just thinking of how Bobby would feel."

"When he's older, he'll understand," Dylan said. "Besides, there's no choice. He violated a court order. You won't really have a say in whether he's prosecuted."

"Not even if I say he had my permission?" she asked, grasping at straws. She knew she was being irrational, that she ought to want him punished, but she just wanted Bobby back. She wanted things to be normal again. It was what she had desperately wanted when she'd moved to Texas, a normal life with her son. She had known then she was taking a risk by making her deal with a man hooked on pills, but it had seemed worth it. Getting out with Bobby had been all that mattered.

Dylan's unflinching gaze remained on her face. "What's really going on, Kelsey? What are you afraid of?"

"I told you, I'm afraid for Bobby, how he'll react to all of this."

Dylan shifted away from her then, his expression blank. Kelsey realized that once more he didn't believe her. She also thought she detected something else in his reaction: hurt. He was hurt, probably disappointed, too, that she didn't trust him with the whole truth.

She hadn't thought she could be any more miserable than she had been ever since Bobby had disappeared, but she was. She felt as if she had let down yet another person in her life. Dylan had been a stranger just a few short days ago, but she already knew that under different circumstances he was someone she would like, someone who deserved better than what she was giving him.

She reached out and laid a hand on his arm, felt the muscle bunch beneath her fingers. "I'm sorry," she said.

"For?"

She shook her head. "Just sorry."

He caught her gaze, held it, then sighed. "Yeah, whatever."

A moment later, he was gone. Kelsey shuddered, feeling a sudden chill in the air that had nothing to do with the air-conditioning. When she'd left Paul, she had made a solemn oath to herself to live without regrets. Now they were piling up faster than she could count them.

Chapter Six

More than ready to be doing something useful, Dylan got as far as the kitchen after walking out on Kelsey. He fully intended to hit the road and join the door-to-door search of hotels and motels, but Lizzy stopped him.

"What's going on? You look mad enough to chew nails."

He jerked his head toward the stairs. "Your friend up there is keeping things from us."

He noticed that Lizzy looked vaguely guilty and seized on it. "You know what she's hiding, don't you? Justin figured you would."

Her chin shot up with a typical touch of Adams defiance. "I have no idea what you're talking about."

"I'm not a fool, Lizzy. Don't you go making the same mistake that Kelsey's making."

"Dylan, of course I don't think you're a fool." She plunged her hands deep into a batch of bread dough, concentrating fully on the task for a moment before she met his gaze again. "Look, this isn't my story to tell."

"Not even to save Bobby?" he asked quietly. "That's what this comes down to, you know. That little boy's life could depend on one of you coming clean with me or with Justin."

That said, he walked out and let the back door slam behind him. Maybe the message would sink in, maybe it wouldn't. Maybe she'd pass it on to Kelsey, maybe she wouldn't. Either way, he'd delivered the warning. It was all he could do, he concluded with frustration. He couldn't beat the rest of the story out of either one of them. He felt his lips curve in a grim smile. He'd leave that to Justin.

Almost an entire day had passed without a single word from Paul and Bobby. Back in the kitchen again after a few hours of restless sleep, Kelsey stared at the phone until her eyes hurt from the strain.

"Eat," Lizzy commanded, putting a loaf of warm bread on the table along with freshly churned butter from the housekeeper at White Pines and a pot of blackberry jam. "I'll have some scrambled eggs for you in a sec."

Kelsey regarded her bleakly. "I'm not hungry."

"Tell someone who cares. Eat, anyway. You have to keep your strength up."

Kelsey stared at Lizzy, shocked by her cool tone. "What's wrong, Lizzy?"

"Oh, not much. A few hours ago I was reamed out by the man we brought in to find Bobby. He all but accused me of standing in the way of Bobby's safe return."

Kelsey stared, openmouthed. "Dylan blamed you?"

"Not for the kidnapping, but for keeping something from him. I wonder where he got the idea there was some big, dark secret?" she asked, staring pointedly at Kelsey.

"Well, I certainly didn't tell him," she retorted, then sighed. "It's just that the man can read me like a book. It's uncanny. Either he's a terrific private eye or..." She stumbled over what she'd been about to say.

"Or there's a connection between the two of you," Lizzy suggested lightly. "I vote for that. I think he's as upset because you don't trust him as he is because there might be something that could help in the search."

Kelsey sighed. "Yes, that was the impression I got, too." She met Lizzy's gaze. "Am I wrong? Would it help to tell him why I think Paul really took Bobby?"

"I honestly don't know," Lizzy said. "But we're not the experts. Only Justin and Dylan know for sure if it would help. Maybe it's time to break your promise to Paul. After all, he hasn't exactly lived up to his end of the bargain."

"I know. I just keep thinking he'll freak if he finds out. Then what?"

"There's no reason for him to find out you've told them. It's not like they're going to announce, hey, buddy, we hear you've been popping too many painkillers and getting them illegally, to boot."

"But they could file charges," Kelsey said.

"He didn't write the forged prescriptions in Texas," Lizzy pointed out. "The crime occurred in another jurisdiction."

"I suppose." She buried her face in her hands. "This is so awful. I never in a million years thought things would come to this when I left Paul. I thought it was over, that he would see that the agreement was in his best interests. He's a brilliant man. His whole career, everything he's worked so hard for, all of it's on the line. How could he be so dumb?"

"Because his brain is clouded by narcotics," Lizzy said flatly. "That's what makes the whole situation so dangerous. He can't possibly be thinking clearly."

She sat down next to Kelsey and grasped her hands. "I think you need to tell Dylan or Justin the whole truth. Now, Kelsey, before something happens and you live to regret it."

She drew in a deep breath, then nodded. "Okay. As soon as Dylan comes back, I'll tell him," she promised.

"You don't want to call him, get him back here?"

"No. He's out looking for Bobby. Maybe he'll find him and all this will become moot."

Lizzy looked as if she was about to argue, but her father's arrival silenced her. "Hey, Daddy," she said, when Harlan Adams rapped on the back door. "Come on in."

He came straight to Kelsey and held out his arms. "How are you, darlin' girl? This must be making you crazy."

"I've had better days," she agreed. "Thanks for stopping by."

"Just wanted to see for myself how you're holding up. Janet says if you need her, just give a shout and she'll come in. She's in the car, but thought you might be getting sick of people hovering."

"Not the two of you," Kelsey said.

"Is my grandson doing right by you?" he asked.

"Justin's been wonderful."

"To tell you the truth, I thought he'd have that boy back by now. Maybe I ought to start making a few calls. I've got some friends around this state who can shake things up."

"Daddy, leave this to Justin," Lizzy said. "He doesn't need you interfering in his work."

Harlan regarded Lizzy indignantly. "Who's interfering? I'm just trying to see that the job gets done." He turned his gaze back to Kelsey. "What about this Delacourt fellow? Is he any good?"

"He seems to be," Kelsey said. "He and Justin have come up with some solid leads. They're checking them out now."

"Tell him to come by the house. I want to meet him, see for myself whether he's up to the job."

"Daddy," Lizzy protested. "You can't cross-examine Dylan. He'll tell you to mind your own damned business."

"If he does, he does. At least I'll have had a look at him. I like that sister of his a lot. She's settled Hardy down, turned him into a regular family man.

Didn't get to see too much of her brothers at the wedding, except to notice that they're a handsome lot. Dark-haired, blue-eyed scoundrels from the look of them. And of course, I know they're from a fine family. Jordan says the Delacourts are honorable people.''

"Well, you would certainly know all about scoundrels, wouldn't you?" Lizzy teased. "Just look at the men in this family."

"Watch your tongue, young lady. I raised fine, honorable sons and a couple of rambunctious daughters. My grandbabies are living up to the same tradition. I won't listen to anyone who says otherwise."

"Because you're prejudiced," she accused.

Kelsey listened to the banter, then chuckled despite the gravity of her own circumstances. "You two are so wonderful," she said. "You might bicker and tease, but there's so much love there. It's the way with your whole family. I want Bobby to grow up feeling that kind of love."

As suddenly as she'd laughed, her voice caught on a sob and the tears flowed again.

Harlan Adams took her hand in his. "He will, darlin' girl. You can count on it. If there's a God in heaven, Bobby will be back here before you know it. Just have faith."

Kelsey wanted desperately to believe him, but right this second her faith was in short supply.

When Justin was parceling out search assignments, Dylan opted for going to scour the Dallas-Fort Worth area. He needed to put some space be-

tween himself and Kelsey James. He was too
irritated with her. He was also undeniably attracted
to her. It was a lousy mix for a situation that required cool, calm objectivity.

Besides, he was itching for action. Some private
investigators could spend all day just doing computer research. Not him. He needed to be on the
move, especially when he had so many reasons for
wanting to succeed.

A part of him wanted to find Paul and Bobby, so
he could be the one to reunite mother and son. Another less attractive part of him wanted to put a fist
in the other man's face. It was a toss-up which part
would win when the moment of truth came.

And there was still a tiny, albeit rapidly fading,
part that hoped the dad made a clean getaway with
his boy. That part made him work all the harder to
find the two of them and get them home.

Armed with pictures of Bobby and Paul, along
with the tag number and description of Paul's car,
plus the Yellow Pages' listings of hotels and motels,
he began making his way around town.

He started with the fancier places first, guessing
that even in a situation like this Paul would want his
creature comforts. From everything he'd learned
from Kelsey, the man was seriously into status. Besides, exclusive, luxury hotels were famed for their
discretion. They might be inclined to ask fewer
questions of their guests as long as their credit cards
had very high limits.

He strode into the lobby of the fifth hotel just as
a man and a boy exited the coffee shop off the
lobby. His pulse leapt. He crossed the lobby in quick

strides, almost panicking when the elevator doors opened before he got there. But the elevator was going down, not up, and the pair waited for the next car.

Dylan edged closer, then took a good hard look. The boy had Bobby's sun-streaked hair, but that's where the similarities ended. The eye color didn't match, the freckles that should have stood out across his nose weren't there. The man regarded Dylan with an open, friendly smile, then turned away as the elevator came.

"You going up?" he asked, holding the door.

Dylan shook his head. "No, sorry. There's something I need to do first."

He headed back to the desk. Here, as at the other hotels, the clerks shook their heads after looking over the pictures.

"Nope. Haven't seen them," the supervisor said. "If you want to wait a minute, I'll compare the tag number to those on file."

"How about letting me do that?" Dylan suggested, offering the man a fifty-dollar bill.

The man pushed it back with obvious regret. "Sorry. It's all on computer, and I can't let you back here."

Dylan nodded. "I'll grab a cup of coffee and come back."

He ate a sandwich while he was at it, though five minutes later he couldn't have said what it was. He kept thinking about the last few minutes he'd spent with Kelsey, about her refusal to trust him. He wasn't sure why that had cut straight through him. He'd tried telling himself it was just because her silence could be keeping him and Justin from finding her kid, but it was more than that. It was personal.

After all, he thought, still vaguely disgruntled, he'd put aside his reservations about her and the whole sole-custody thing. He'd respected her feelings, listened to her, but when push came to shove, she wasn't willing to return that same level of trust.

Why? he wondered. Just because he was a man and her ex-husband had turned her off men? Or was it about him, some innate distrust of him specifically?

Or was it as simple as fear? Was whatever she was hiding so devastating that she felt she didn't dare reveal it? What could be that bad?

He went over it and over it and couldn't come up with a thing. What could a woman like Kelsey James, a brilliant doctor from all reports, have to hide? Or was it her ex's secrets?

Damn, this was getting him nowhere. He went back to the desk where the supervisor told him he hadn't been able to find a match for the tag number. Dylan gave him his card. "Call me if anything turns up, okay?"

"Absolutely. I have kids of my own. I can't imagine what that mother must be feeling."

"She's terrified," Dylan said succinctly.

"Well, I'll keep my eyes open. You can count on that."

Dylan nodded and set off for the next hotel on his list. He was running out of big, impersonal hotels. A few more and he'd be down to the moderately priced chains. There were a lot of them, scattered from one end of Dallas to the other with more in Fort Worth. Maybe he should just take a page out of Becky's book, find a room for himself and settle down with a phone. He could call faster than he could visit. It was a less time-consuming form of legwork, even if it was less likely to put a dent in his restless energy.

He booked a room near the airport, ordered up a pot of coffee, then settled down at the desk. The first call he made wasn't to a hotel on the list, but to Kelsey. Most clients didn't get frequent updates, didn't expect them, but this case was different and not just because she was a terror-stricken mom, either. It was because he had the unmistakable feeling that she was the kind of woman who could matter to him, a disconcerting discovery in the middle of a kidnapping investigation, especially when there was so much distrust between them.

"Hey, Kelsey," he said when she snatched up the phone on the first ring.

"Dylan? Where are you?"

He tried not to sigh at the eagerness in her voice. It wasn't for him. It was for news of Bobby. There was no point in lying to himself about that. "In Dallas, checking out the hotels."

"Anything?"

"No. Sorry, darlin'. Anything turn up back there? Any calls from Paul?"

The question was greeted by silence.

"Kelsey?"

"Oh, sorry. No. I was shaking my head, but I guess you couldn't know that," she said wryly. "I'm not thinking very clearly."

"You're excused." He fell silent himself, aware that he had nothing more to say that she really wanted to hear and that they were tying up the line as well. "Listen, I'll check in with you every so often. You hang in there, okay?"

"I'm doing the best I can. And Dylan…"

"Yes?"

"When you get back, we need to talk."

"About?"

"We'll discuss it when you get here," she said. "Face-to-face."

So, he thought, staring at the phone after they'd hung up, she was going to share her secret, after all. He couldn't help wondering if it was worth dropping everything to go straight home to hear.

Then again, maybe he could get through with these calls in record time and be back in Los Piños before daybreak. His spirits brightened at the prospect. He figured the reasons for *that* didn't bear close examination.

"Daddy, I want to play outside," Bobby pleaded for the tenth time in as many minutes.

"No," Paul said, clinging to his patience by a thread.

"I don't like it in here. It smells funny."

The room did have the musty smell of smoke and old furniture that had absorbed the scents of too many guests. Paul doubted it had had a good cleaning in months, if not years. Normally he wouldn't have set foot in a dive like this, but he figured the police would be looking for him in the big, fancy hotels he tended to favor. Besides, he'd discovered that there were a lot of small, out-of-the-way motels in Texas where a man could buy silence. He only needed a few more days. By then, he was pretty sure Kelsey would agree to anything he asked.

"Why can't we go out?" Bobby asked.

"Because I said so," Paul snapped. "Watch TV."

"No," Bobby said with a stubborn tilt to his chin. "It's all fuzzy. Want to play catch."

"Not now."

"When?"

"Later."

"When is later?"

Paul sighed. This was harder than he'd anticipated. Entertaining a three-year-old was time-consuming work. He'd forgotten that. It wasn't like he didn't have other things on his mind, either.

"Look, son, I'll get you some books next time I go out. You can look at the pictures, okay?"

"I like *my* books. Call Mommy. She knows which books I like."

"We are not calling your mother."

"Why?" Bobby's eyes filled with tears. "I miss Mommy. Why can't she come with us?"

"Because she's a very busy doctor and this is just a guy trip. You and me, buddy. Okay?"

Bobby heaved a sigh, then curled into a ball on the bed, looking miserable. Paul regarded him with real regret and heaved a sigh of his own.

Then he reached for the bottle containing his last few pills.

Chapter Seven

He must have made a hundred phone calls, all without picking up so much as a whiff of Paul James and Bobby, Dylan thought, slamming the motel phone down in disgust. He was wasting time. He might as well head back to Los Piños, which he'd wanted to do the night before. Kelsey finally appeared to be in a talkative mood. Maybe he'd get something out of a heart-to-heart with her. He could be there in a few hours, longer if he stopped to check the guest registers of any motels he passed along the way.

He punched in the number for the Los Piños sheriff's office and got Becky on the line. "Any news?"

"Nothing," she said, sounding as exhausted as he felt.

"There's nothing here, either. I'm coming back. Let Justin know, okay?"

"Will do. Gotta run. There's another call coming in."

"Thanks, Becky. See you soon."

He made one last call, this time to Trish. "Hey, sis."

"Dylan, where on earth have you been? I've been worried sick."

"Why?" he asked, not used to anyone worrying about him. It had been a long time. After a couple of years, Kit had given up asking about his schedule. She'd said she was tired of his insensitivity. He'd accused her of nagging. In fact, that had been the beginning of the end of their marriage.

"I thought you'd at least check in last night," Trish scolded.

"Sorry. As soon as I was assigned to do a quick search in the Dallas-Fort Worth area, I took off. It never even occurred to me to call you."

"I think I'm beginning to see why Kit complained so bitterly," his sister said mildly. "You get so caught up in the hunt, you forget all about the people who love you."

"Okay, Trish. I get it. I'm sorry."

"Good. Now, tell me, did you find anything? When are you coming back?"

"Nothing," he said for the second time that morning. "And I should be back in a few hours. Do me a favor."

"Anything," she said at once.

"Call Jeb and see what he's got going on at work.

Tell him I could use him on this, if he can get away.''

''You want me to get our brother to come to Los Piños and help you on a case? Won't Father have a cow?''

Dylan chuckled. ''I certainly hope so. I try to stick it to him whenever I can. Jeb's a better P.I. than he is an oilman and everyone except Dad knows it.''

''You're kidding,'' Trish said, clearly amazed. ''He's worked with you before?''

''Every chance he gets,'' Dylan told her.

''What about Michael and Tyler?''

''No, I am very much afraid that neither of them will leave the family business, though Tyler is showing evidence that he'd like to slip out of a suit and tie and go work the rigs. Dad hasn't quite decided how he feels about that one yet.''

''How come I didn't know about any of this?''

''Because you were too busy with your own rebellion.''

''Yes,'' she agreed thoughtfully. ''I suppose I was. Okay, I'll call Jeb. Anything else?''

''Nope. Just pray that today's the day we get a break. I don't like the way this is dragging on. I want that boy back home, where he belongs.''

He heard Trish's quiet intake of breath.

''Dylan, does that mean you're really okay with the fact that she's got full custody? There's not a part of you hoping that Paul will get away with Bobby?''

''Not anymore,'' he said, praying he was being truthful.

"You're sure?" she persisted.

"I have to accept that Bobby's with her for a reason. I just wish to hell someone would come clean and tell me what it is. See you later, sis. I will check in. I promise."

"You'd better, or I'll tell Laura that her favorite uncle is a perfect example of the kind of man she should steer clear of."

"That might be good advice under any circumstances," he admitted. "Just don't lay it on her now."

"Don't give me any reason to," she countered. "Love you."

Dylan smiled as he hung up. He really needed to spend more time counting his blessings. Trish and Laura would be at the top of the list, sharing first place. His brothers—especially Jeb—ranked a close second. They were the people he'd always known he could count on. Just like the Adamses, they were fiercely loyal, strong-willed and honorable.

And Dr. Kelsey James? The thought popped into his head, startling him. Where had that come from? His libido, no doubt. He'd have to find some way to deal with that when this was all over. For now, though, he definitely needed to table it.

That was easier said than done, he concluded when he walked into her house just after noon and found her on her hands and knees scrubbing the kitchen floor, her sexy little butt poked in the air, and a pair of shorts exposing way too many inches of her legs. Her sleeveless T-shirt had crawled up her back, leaving her midriff bare. He sucked in a deep breath and tried to tame his wildly errant thoughts.

"It's a little late in the year for spring-cleaning, isn't it?" he suggested. He spoke quietly, but startled her just the same. She jumped, knocking over the pail of sudsy water beside her. Her gaze shot up.

"You," she exclaimed as if he'd been an unwelcome thief. "Look what you made me do."

"Tell me where to look and I'll get a mop."

"Never mind. I'll clean it up as I go."

Dylan let it pass. He circled the spreading puddle of water, grabbed a chair and sat down to watch. He could see that the scrubbing and regaining her composure were giving her an equally difficult time.

"Don't mind me," she said eventually. "Sitting around waiting was driving me nuts. When I'm upset, I clean. If this drags on much longer, the house will be spotless."

"Paul hasn't called today?"

She shook her head, then rocked back on her haunches to meet his gaze. "He's doing it deliberately," she said bitterly. "He wants me to suffer."

"Why? Because you divorced him?"

"Maybe."

Dylan had a hunch that was only part of the story. "Why did you leave him?"

"It wasn't working out."

"Kelsey," he chided. "I thought you were going to talk to me when I got back. I'm here now. Let's have the whole story."

A wave of something that might have been shame washed over her face. "It's just so ugly," she began, then stopped when the phone rang. Clearly relieved at the interruption, she grabbed for the portable phone sitting on a nearby chair.

"Yes?"

Dylan couldn't hear what was said, but something in her expression told him all he needed to know.

"Paul?" he mouthed.

She nodded. "Let me talk to Bobby," she said, as Dylan slipped into the living room to pick up the extension there.

"Mommy?"

The tentative little voice tugged at Dylan's heart. Did every little kid sound like that on the phone? Would Shane if he could hear him?

"Hi, baby," Kelsey said, the upbeat note in her voice clearly forced. "How're you doing?"

"I wanna come home, Mommy. I miss you."

"I miss you, too, sweetie. You'll be home soon. Are you having fun with Daddy?"

"Uh-uh," Bobby complained. "He won't let me go outside. He bringed me hamburgers and French fries for lunch and dinner every day. Don't want hamburgers anymore."

"I thought you loved hamburgers," Kelsey said to him, responding to the petulance with a teasing tone. "You always grumble that I never buy you hamburgers."

"No more," he said adamantly. "Want pizza and ice cream."

"Well, maybe Daddy will get that for you tonight. Let me talk to him again, okay?"

Dylan heard the exchange between Bobby and his father, then Paul snapped, "Yes?"

"Bring him back, Paul."

"Just like that? I don't think so."

"When?"

"You'll be hearing from me," he said and hung up.

Dylan slowly replaced the receiver, still struck by the tension and anger in Paul's voice. If he'd ever doubted that this was about something besides a dad wanting to be with his son, he had his proof now. Paul wasn't making the most of this chance to be with Bobby. They weren't bonding, making up for lost time. Paul was all but holding his son captive for reasons that weren't yet clear to Dylan.

No, this was definitely about something between Paul and Kelsey. It was a power play, Dylan concluded.

He walked slowly back into the kitchen and found Kelsey sitting right where he'd left her, holding the phone and staring at it dejectedly.

She glanced up. "You heard?"

"Most of it." He hunkered down beside her, took the phone and set it back on the chair. "You okay?"

She gazed at him, fire flaring in her eyes, just as he'd hoped it would.

"Of course I'm not okay. My ex-husband has my son and is using him to play some kind of sick game with me. How could I possibly be okay?" she demanded in a voice that shook with fury.

Dylan reached for her just as the sobs started. Like a child seeking the comfort of a parent's embrace, she came willingly into his arms. Dylan held her and rocked her, feeling the tight knot of blame and resentment that had been inside him from the beginning of this case slowly ease. This was Kelsey, not Kit, and despite the odds against it, she was growing dear to him. So was a little boy he'd never even met. Hearing Bobby's voice had made him more real than ever.

Dylan knew he was still missing critical pieces of the puzzle, but it didn't seem to matter so much anymore. Beyond the tension and anger, he hadn't liked what he'd heard in Paul's voice. The man was a bully.

Plus, seeing that haunted look in Kelsey's eyes, hearing her little boy beg to come home were enough to convince him that Bobby belonged here, and the sooner he was back, the better. If there were legal issues to be resolved, they could be sorted out later.

He tipped Kelsey's chin up, until their gazes clashed. "We will get Bobby back," he told her firmly. "Soon."

"I'm so afraid," she whispered, tears still spilling down her cheeks.

"Don't be," he whispered, pressing a kiss to her forehead. She trembled. Lost in the shimmering, expressive depths of her eyes, Dylan shuddered as well. Wanting only to give comfort, he touched his lips to her cheek in another kiss, tasted salty tears, then without thinking he moved on to her mouth.

Her lips parted beneath his, welcomed him, but with a desperation born of circumstances, not passion for him. He doubted she was even aware of who held her, conscious only of the need to be held, the yearning to feel alive instead of dead inside. He knew because in the first weeks after Shane was gone for good, he had tried losing himself in a succession of meaningless encounters. It hadn't worked for him. It surely wouldn't for Kelsey.

Finally he pulled back, rested his forehead against hers, and let his breathing slow to normal. And then he carefully withdrew, the act both physical and emotional. He retreated, praying he could hang on to his professional objectivity just a little longer, just until Bobby was safely home again.

Kelsey obviously didn't understand what was going on. She stared at him in confusion. "Why?"

"Not now, Kelsey. It's not the time."

A shudder washed over her, as if she had suddenly become aware of what she'd been about to do. "Oh, God, what was I thinking?"

"You weren't," he said dryly. "Neither was I. We were feeling." He forced her gaze to his. "And that's okay, Kelsey. In fact, it's more than okay. I promise you, we'll get back to it, when the time is right."

A blush stained her cheeks and she gave him a smile that wobbled. "You think?"

"Oh, yes, darlin'. I can all but guarantee it," he said fervently. "Now let me get Lizzy or somebody else over here to stay with you, so I can get back on the job."

"I'll be fine by myself. I don't need somebody hovering."

"I think you do," he said, just as firmly.

But in the end, he couldn't track Lizzy down, so he called Trish. "Can you come over and spend some time with Kelsey?"

"Of course," she said at once. "I'll be right

there.'' She hesitated. ''Dylan, what about Laura? Should I bring her or find a sitter?''

He knew exactly what she meant. Having a baby around right now might be more than Kelsey could bear. ''A sitter, I think.''

''No,'' Kelsey said at once, obviously guessing the topic. ''Tell her to bring Laura. Seeing that precious girl will do me a world of good. It'll remind me of what I'm fighting to get back.''

Dylan regarded her worriedly. ''Are you sure?''

''Absolutely.''

He nodded. ''Trish, bring the munchkin. Kelsey wants her here.''

''Will do. By the way, I spoke to Jeb. He's on his way. You were right. He was downright eager to get out from under Dad's thumb.''

Dylan laughed. ''At this rate, dear old Dad is going to have to come to Los Piños, if he expects to see his kids again.''

''Does that mean you're thinking of sticking around?'' Trish asked.

Dylan's gaze sought out Kelsey, who was busying herself putting the sponges and bucket away. ''We'll see, sis. You know me. I take life the same way I build a case, one step at a time.''

''Not that you asked, but nothing would make me happier than to have those steps lead you here.''

''We'll see,'' he said, as Kelsey turned and met his gaze. He hung up the phone, then repeated the words for Kelsey's benefit. ''We'll see.''

He gave her a wink and headed for the door. ''Trish will be here soon. If a rogue who looks a lot like me turns up here, don't let him in. Send him straight to the sheriff's office.''

She regarded him quizzically. ''Is that because he belongs in jail?''

''A few days in lockup probably wouldn't hurt him,'' he said. ''But actually, it'll be my brother Jeb looking for me. I asked him to come and help out.''

''One more thing to thank you for,'' she murmured. ''How will I ever repay you?''

''Oh, I'm sure, when the time comes, we'll think of something. Meantime, keep that chin up.''

Kelsey couldn't believe how much Dylan had become a part of her life. He was rapidly becoming her linchpin, her tower of strength. Despite those early misgivings, she was sure that he was fully and completely on her side now.

Under other circumstances, she might have joked with Lizzy about what a hunk he was, but now she hated herself for even noticing. And, of course, there had been that kiss. She wasn't entirely sure how it had started, but, holy kamoley, there was no mistaking how it could have ended. How she had wanted it to end.

What on earth was wrong with her? How could she be attracted to Dylan—to anyone—when her boy was missing? How could she have considered, even for a second, just giving in to passion and letting it wipe out the pain, even temporarily?

Normally he wasn't the sort of man who'd even notice her, but she could tell that he did. But just when she thought she detected a male-female sort of heat in his gaze, he withdrew to that distant place where she couldn't reach him. He'd done it after that kiss, despite his reassurances that they'd get back to it another time.

Her skin was still burning, just as it had to his touch, when Trish knocked at the back door. "Okay to come in?"

"Absolutely," Kelsey told her, relieved to have the distraction. She caught sight of Laura clinging to her mother's hand and knelt down. "Hey, you. How about a cookie?"

Laura's eyes brightened. "Cookie?" she said at once, her head bobbing eagerly. Then she cast a cautious glance at her mother. "'Kay, Mama?"

"Yes, it's okay. But just one," Trish said. "Then you have to lie down on the sofa and take a nap."

"Nap," Laura echoed dutifully, already reaching for the oatmeal-raisin cookie Kelsey was holding out.

"Want to bet she forgets all about that nap when the time comes?" Trish said. She touched Kelsey's cheek. "How are you holding up?"

"By a thread," Kelsey said honestly. "Your brother has been amazing. He's been working on this nonstop."

Trish seemed about to say something, then caught herself.

"What?" Kelsey prodded.

"Nothing."

"I thought we knew each other well enough to speak our minds," Kelsey scolded. "You don't have to censor yourself with me."

Trish still seemed hesitant. "I just don't think I

should get into this. Dylan wouldn't want me saying anything.''

''About?'' Kelsey asked, then waited.

''It's just that this has been incredibly hard on him,'' Trish said finally.

Puzzled, Kelsey stared. ''Why? I'm sure he's a caring man who'd be upset to see anyone suffering, but you make it sound as if something more is going on.''

Trish hesitated.

''You're making me nervous, Trish. What don't I know?''

''Did you know he has a little boy of his own?''

Kelsey was stunned. Dylan had never mentioned him. ''No. He hasn't said a word.''

''He doesn't talk much about Shane.''

He certainly hadn't said anything to her, she thought, hurt by the omission. How could he not share something so personal with her, especially in the past day or two when they'd been getting closer?

''Why?'' she asked Trish.

''Because he gave up custody. Shane is with Dylan's ex and her new husband. He pretty much tries to pretend his son doesn't exist, but it tears him up inside that Kit has the boy and he never sees him.''

In that instant Kelsey realized why Dylan had kept his distance, why disdain had once crept in just when she thought they were getting closer.

''I see,'' she said, fighting the feeling that she'd been had, that he had betrayed her. It wasn't an entirely rational reaction, given how hard he'd been working for her and the secret she had deliberately kept from him, but that didn't seem to matter. She had to wonder just how hard he really had been working. Had he only been going through the motions, because it was expected of him by people who *did* matter to him?

Trish studied her worriedly. "I've made it worse, haven't I? I knew I should keep my mouth shut. Now you don't trust him. This is exactly what Dylan was worried about."

"I do have to wonder whose side he's really on."

"Yours," Trish said adamantly. "He would never let his personal feelings interfere in a case."

"I should have known about this, just the same."

"I agree," Trish said. "I told him to tell you."

"Then why didn't he?"

"He said he needed you to trust him, if he was going to help you."

"He was right about that," Kelsey said coolly. "I need to trust him."

Trish squeezed her hand. "You can, you know."

Kelsey shook her head. "I don't think so."

Numb, she fell silent. A short time later, she made an excuse that she had a raging headache and sent Trish away. Then she called Dylan at the sheriff's office.

"I want to see you," she said, when he came on the line.

"Can it wait?"

"I don't think so."

"Has Paul called again?"

"No. Just come, Dylan. Now."

Something in her voice must have alerted him that she was in no mood for excuses, because he said quietly, "I'll be right there."

When he came in, she studied his face, trying to read the truth. What were his real motivations in taking this case? Had he already betrayed her? Had he deliberately let Paul slip away? Was he eager to see another dad succeed where he had failed?

"What's wrong?" he asked.

She put it bluntly. "Are you really on my side or Paul's?"

He looked wounded by the question. "Where did that come from?"

"Trish told me about your little boy."

He went absolutely still, then stood up and began to pace.

"Well, was she lying?"

"No, of course not, but she had no right to tell you about that."

Kelsey steeled herself against the pain in his eyes. "I'm glad she did. It was about time somebody filled me in. I had a right to know that you might have divided loyalties. Now answer me. Whose side are you on?"

He hesitated for no more than an instant, but it was long enough to infuriate her, long enough to condemn him in her eyes.

"You're fired," she told him. "I don't want you working on this anymore."

"Kelsey—"

She cut off the protest. "No. You've probably helped him get away."

"Why would I do that?" he asked reasonably. "I'm working for you. My professional reputation wouldn't be worth spit if I let my own feelings interfere in a case I'd accepted. Believe me, if I felt that strongly about your situation, I would never have taken the case in the first place.''

"You were under a lot of pressure to take it," she pointed out. "Lizzy asked. Trish lives here in town. You probably felt you owed it to them."

He ran his fingers through his hair. "Okay, yes. I did feel I owed them, but there was never a time when I couldn't have called in another investigator if I'd thought it would be for the best.''

"But isn't that just the point?'' she demanded. "Best for whom? Me or Paul?'' Even as she said it, she knew she was beyond reason. She'd been wanting somebody to blame for days now and Dylan was right here. He was an easier target than Paul.

"Okay, I'll ask you again," he said with exaggerated patience. "Why would I do that?''

His mild tone which suggested he was merely tolerating her outburst incensed her. She lashed out again. "Because your ex-wife has sole custody of your son and you haven't forgiven her for it. You're getting even with her through me.''

"She has sole custody because I made the decision that it was for the best.''

"So you say.''

Dylan flinched under the bitter assault, but he didn't argue with her. He let it drop, accepting her judgment, obviously because she'd hit on the truth. He *was* on Paul's side. And for that, Kelsey was certain she would never be able to forgive him.

Later, when her temper had cooled and she could think back on the conversation rationally, she realized that at that moment, it looked as if a light in Dylan's eyes had gone out. She ached for the unfair accusations she had hurled at him, but it was too late to take them back.

By then he was gone and she was all alone. Completely alone. The silence was deafening.

Only then did she hear the tiny, nagging voice in her head all but shouting that she had just made the worst mistake of her life.

Chapter Eight

Dylan dropped into a chair in Trish's living room without even bothering to turn on the light. He was too exhausted to move, too drained to even drag himself off to bed. Kelsey's charge that he'd let her down because of sympathy for her ex hadn't been nearly as unfounded as he would have liked.

Oh, he had done his best to find Bobby. He'd left no stone unturned, no lead ignored, but he couldn't honestly say he'd done it with enthusiasm. Not in the beginning. True, he had wanted Bobby reunited with his mother, a woman he'd come to care about more than he wanted to admit. But at the father's expense? Even now, when he knew in his gut it was the right thing to do, the idea still brought up more bitter memories than he'd ever wanted to revisit. That was why he hadn't been able to argue with the damning conclusions Kelsey had obviously jumped to.

He was still sitting there when Trish came downstairs at dawn to fix breakfast for Hardy, who was splitting his days between duties at the ranch and search parties that continued to comb half of West Texas looking for some trace of Paul James and Bobby.

"Dylan, what are you doing sitting down here in the dark?" She stepped into the room and took a closer look. "You look like hell."

"Feel like it, too."

"What time did you get in last night? I never heard you."

He shrugged. He hadn't looked at his watch. After he'd left Kelsey's, he'd driven around for hours, then instinctively stopped in at the sheriff's office to check in with Justin. There had been no news, no leads.

Trish sat down opposite him. "Okay, big brother, spill it. What's wrong?"

"Aside from the fact that here's no sign of Bobby and the fact that I've been fired? Aside from those two things, I'd say life is just about perfect."

Trish stared at him with undisguised astonishment. "Fired? Why?"

"Your friend seems to think I might have a conflict of interest. I don't suppose you're the one who mentioned Shane to her."

His sister flushed guiltily. "Yes, and I could see she was overreacting, but I thought I'd calmed her down. I had no idea she'd go off the deep end. You've worked your tail off on this case. How dare she fire you?'' she asked indignantly. ''Don't worry, Dylan. I'll talk to her.''

''No need. I'm not going to stop working, just because of a little technicality like being fired. I wasn't planning on getting paid anyway. Are you going over there today?''

She nodded. ''Right after breakfast.''

''Do something for me.''

''Anything.''

''See if you can find out what she's holding back. There's something she hasn't told me. She almost let it out yesterday, but then Paul called and we got sidetracked. Before that she clammed up whenever I asked. I know she won't tell me now, but I have a feeling it's crucial.''

''Maybe Lizzy knows. Have you talked to her?''

''I tried. She was as evasive as hell, too.''

''I'll do what I can.''

''Thanks. I'm going to go up and grab a shower. Think you can have some lethally strong coffee ready when I get back down?''

''You got it, big brother.'' She gave him a hug. ''Don't let what Kelsey did get you down. She appreciates your help and she cares about you. I know she does.''

''Sure,'' he said grimly, thinking of the way she'd kissed him, the way she'd melted in his arms. She cared, all right. ''She just doesn't trust me.''

When he came back down, feeling marginally better after an icy shower, he found not only Hardy at the kitchen table with Trish, but Jeb. His brother, who was only a year younger, frowned at him.

''For a man in such a big hurry to get me over

here, you might have stuck around last night to tell me what you need me to do,'' Jeb noted without any real venom, spooning cereal into his mouth as if he hadn't had a meal in a month.

Dylan winced. "Sorry. I got sidetracked."

Jeb stared, clearly incredulous. "You? In the middle of a case?" He turned his gaze on Trish. "Did I miss the sky falling?"

"Very funny," Dylan retorted. "Now if you're finished trying to eat Trish and Hardy out of house and home, we can hit the road."

"Oh, no, you don't," Trish said, motioning toward a chair. "Sit. You're not leaving here until you've had coffee and breakfast. I'll make you an omelet."

Dylan knew better than to argue. Trish could nag worse than their mother, if she put her mind to it. Besides, he knew she wanted badly to make up for spilling the beans to Kelsey about Shane.

"I'll take the coffee and some toast. That's enough."

"You'll eat eggs and be grateful for them," she countered, whipping the eggs with a whisk. She poured them into a pan sizzling with melted butter. "Jeb might be able to run all day on a sugar high, but you need protein."

Hardy grinned at the display of bossiness. "You're the ones who spoiled her. Thanks to you, she thinks she's queen of the universe," he reminded them. "Now it's time for payback. I think I'll just be running along while all her attention is focused on the two of you."

Trish frowned at her husband with mock severity. "You'll pay for that remark later."

He gave her a hard kiss. "I'll be looking forward to it, darlin'." He winked at Dylan and Jeb. "See. Marriage has its rewards. You might want to consider it."

"The man has all the fervor of a recent convert," Dylan noted to no one in particular.

Jeb shuddered. "Marriage is definitely not for me. Women change once they get a ring on their finger. I've seen it too often not to believe in the phenomenon."

Dylan didn't really want to get drawn into that particular discussion. He concentrated all of his attention on the food Trish had put in front of him. He couldn't help noting, though, that an image of Kelsey popped into his head at the mere mention of marriage.

"Hey, Dylan, I don't hear you swearing off marriage," Jeb said, studying him curiously. "Is something going on over here I don't know about?"

"Nothing," he said tersely, fully aware of the long, speculative look that his brother exchanged with Trish. He threw down his fork. "That's it. Let's get out of here."

Jeb grinned at Trish as he dutifully stood up. "Guess I touched a nerve."

"And if you've got a grain of sense in that hard head of yours, you'll leave it be," Dylan snapped back.

Jeb's hoot of laughter trailed him to the car. He was inside with the motor running before his brother cracked open the door. "Is it safe?"

"As safe as it's going to get."

Jeb climbed in, snapped on his seat belt, then slid down in the seat before glancing over to gauge Dylan's mood. "Does this pleasant frame of mind have something to do with the case or with the beautiful mother?"

Dylan's frown deepened. "How do you know she's beautiful?"

"Where you're concerned, they always are."

"Meaning?" Dylan asked darkly.

"Nothing. Absolutely nothing."

Dylan wasn't buying the denial. "Are you suggesting I'm shallow?"

His brother heaved a sigh. "Okay, you asked for this. Under normal circumstances, no, you are not shallow. But ever since Kit divorced you, you've been more interested in beauty than brains. You haven't exactly been looking for anybody with real staying power. Now that may be okay for me. I'm not the happily-ever-after type. But you're different. You want a home and a family. That's what you deserve. Unfortunately, Kit did a real number on you and threw you off your stride. But this love-'em-and-leave-'em stuff is not you, Dylan. Your middle name should have been dependable."

Dylan had had enough. "How the hell did we get off on this tangent, anyway?" he asked moodily. "I didn't have you come over here to discuss my love life."

"Hitting a little too close to home, am I?" Jeb countered. His expression turned thoughtful. "Maybe I guessed wrong about what's going on here. This Kelsey is a pediatrician, isn't she? Must be smart. Probably has some real substance to her. Am I right?''

"What you are is a pain in the neck.''

"Ah, brains and beauty,'' Jeb concluded triumphantly. "Now we're talking.''

"Do I need to remind you that the woman's child is missing? We haven't exactly been taking time out for a hot romance.''

Jeb studied him. "But you have kissed her, haven't you?''

Dylan felt heat climbing into his cheeks.

Jeb hooted. "I knew it.''

"I am calling Dad first chance I get and telling him you're just itching to have more responsibility at the oil company,'' Dylan vowed. "I might even recommend he make you vice president of something that will require oodles and oodles of paperwork, something with lots and lots of numbers.''

Unfortunately, his brother didn't seem the least bit daunted by the threat.

"Dad knows perfectly well I can't add without a calculator. He still has the accountant go over my checkbook because it's such a mess. He's not about to leave the company finances in my hands.''

Dylan sighed. "You have a point. Okay, enough sparring. Let's talk about Paul James and where he could be hiding with his son.''

Jeb promptly straightened in his seat. "Tell me what you know,'' he said with an eagerness he never displayed when talking about his work for the family oil business.

Dylan laid out the case point by point. For all of his carefree ways, Jeb had a quick mind. They were a good match. Dylan relished the details, the assembling of clues. Jeb could lay them out and see the big picture. When Dylan was finished, Jeb nodded.

"He wants something from Kelsey," he concluded. "And he's stringing her along until he figures she'll be desperate enough to give it to him."

"But what?" Dylan asked. "Obviously not Bobby. He has him and he hasn't made a run for it. I heard him on the phone. I don't even think it's a play to get shared custody. It's something else."

"Money?" Jeb suggested.

Dylan considered it, then shook his head. "Kelsey's not rich. She's a small-town doctor. She probably has medical school bills left to pay. Besides, from what I gathered, Paul is a hotshot stockbroker. He's the one with the bucks."

"Maybe he played fast and loose with his ethics and got himself fired."

"So he stole his kid to get back his credibility?" Dylan asked doubtfully. "I don't think so. Besides, Justin talked to his boss. He's expecting him back after his two-week vacation ends."

"Maybe he's just trying to jerk Kelsey's chain. Maybe this is payback for her leaving him."

Dylan had certainly heard enough taunting animosity in Paul's voice to believe him capable of that kind of cruelty, but it still didn't ring true. He couldn't quite put his finger on why he felt that so strongly. "No," he said eventually. "It's something else. And my gut tells me that Kelsey knows exactly what it is."

"Then let's go see the beautiful pediatrician," Jeb suggested. "We can play good cop, bad cop with her. I'll be the bad guy, since you want to have a future with her when this is all over."

"I never said—"

"You didn't have to, big brother. It's written all over your face. You're the transparent one, remember? That's why Mom always knew you were the one who stole the cookies."

"No, she knew that because the rest of you blabbed," Dylan countered. "But you're right about going to see Kelsey. It's time to put an end to the evasiveness."

"Don't forget, though, I get to be the bad cop," Jeb said.

If the situation hadn't been so deadly serious, Dylan would have laughed at his brother's eagerness. Jeb had obviously spent far to many hours watching shows like *NYPD Blue*. He had the typical amateur's illusions about the glamour of police and detective work. And because he only popped in and out of Dylan's cases at the most critical junctures, he had no idea how much nitty-gritty, boring legwork was required to get to that point.

Dylan approached Kelsey's house with mounting trepidation. After all, she had fired him the night before. He doubted she was going to be overjoyed to find him still at work. Maybe the way around that would be to explain he had brought Jeb in as his replacement. Maybe she wouldn't recall that Jeb had already been on his way to town before Dylan had been fired.

Women tended to accept his brother at face value. Jeb was a charmer with the kind of friendly, open demeanor that drew them in droves. They also tended to take advantage of his good nature, which Dylan believed was the reason Jeb refused to take any relationship seriously. He'd been burned so many times that he now made it a point to be the first to walk away.

"Why is it you look as though we're about to stroll innocently into the lion's den?" Jeb asked as they exited the car. "I thought you liked this woman."

"I'm not exactly at the top of her hit parade at the moment," Dylan admitted, surprised that Trish hadn't explained the situation. "The truth is, she fired me last night."

"She fired you," Jeb echoed, shaking his head. "Now's a fine time to mention that. Maybe you'd better be the bad cop, after all."

Dylan chuckled. "Nah. You do it so well."

He rang the bell and waited. When Lizzy opened the door, she regarded him with shock. "I thought you'd been—"

"Fired?" Dylan supplied.

She nodded.

"I was," he replied cheerfully. "So I hired him." He gestured over his shoulder. "You remember my brother Jeb."

Lizzy stared. "Jeb. Of course. I thought you were in the oil business."

"I'm a man of many talents," he said. "Dylan likes to call on me when he's in over his head."

"Very funny," Dylan muttered. He stepped past Lizzy. "Where's Kelsey?"

"In the kitchen. I'll get her."

"Never mind," Jeb said. "We'll go in there."

"Don't mind him," Dylan said. "He's hoping there will be leftovers from breakfast. He's a bottomless pit."

"Then he's in luck. I've been baking again. Cinnamon rolls this time. It keeps my mind off of things and I keep hoping the aroma of all that sugar and cinnamon will get to Kelsey so she'll eat something."

"She's still not eating?" Dylan asked.

"Not so you'd notice. And she can't afford to lose any weight," Lizzy said.

Dylan thoroughly surveyed Kelsey when he walked into the kitchen and spotted her bent over, scrubbing out the refrigerator. Obviously, she was on another cleaning binge. He found himself agreeing with Lizzy. Even after a few days, her clothes were looser. More important, when she glanced up, her face looked drawn and pale.

Seeing him, though, put bright patches of color on her cheeks, right along with a frown. Dylan badly wanted to kiss her to heighten that color even more, but decided against it. To many fascinated onlookers. Instead, he opted for going on the offensive before she got any brilliant ideas about tossing him right back out the door. He pulled out a chair, then gestured toward it.

"Have a seat," he suggested.

Kelsey didn't budge. In fact, her chin lifted a defiant notch. She pinned his brother with a look. "Who is he?"

"This is my brother. Jeb, this is Dr. Kelsey James."

"I'm sorry about your little boy," Jeb said.

"Thank you." Her gaze shifted back to Dylan. "I thought I'd made myself clear last night. I don't want you on this case."

"Which is why Jeb is stepping in."

"He's a private investigator, too?"

"Part-time," Jeb said, before Dylan could respond. "I ask the tough questions that Dylan's too nice to ask."

She blinked rapidly at that. "Oh?" she said, visibly nervous.

Jeb nodded, his expression still deceptively cheerful. "Such as, what is your ex-husband really after?"

"Excuse me?" Kelsey's voice faltered. She sank onto the chair Dylan was holding. "I'm not sure I understand."

"Sure you do," Jeb corrected. "You're a smart woman. It's bound to have occurred to you that your ex-husband hasn't taken Bobby so he can bond with the boy or go off on some grand adventure."

"I suppose," she admitted grudgingly.

"Well, then, why has he taken him?"

"Because he's not a very nice man," Kelsey snapped.

"I think we can all agree to that," Dylan said. He rested a hand on Kelsey's shoulder. The muscles were tight with tension. His touch didn't seem to be helping. If anything, she stiffened more.

"Does he want money?" Jeb persisted. "After all, you're a doctor. You're friends with the most important family in town. He's got to figure you'd be good for some cash."

"This isn't about money," Kelsey said tersely.

The quick negative responses proved to Dylan that she knew exactly what Paul *did* want.

"But you do have something he wants, don't you?" Jeb prodded.

His gaze met hers with the kind of direct, penetrating stare that few people could ignore. Kelsey was no exception. Dylan felt her tremble, even though she held her own gaze defiantly steady.

"Don't mistake me for my brother, Kelsey," Jeb said, his gaze hardening. "I'm not going to let you off the hook. I'm going to come at this from a hundred different directions, if that's what it takes to get you to open up. We'll try the direct approach one more time. What does Paul James want from you in return for giving back your son?"

A tear spilled from Kelsey's eyes and rolled down her cheek. Lizzy jumped up. "That's enough," she said. "Leave her alone. She's not on trial here. Can't you see you're just upsetting her more? Hasn't she already been through enough?"

Dylan felt some of the tension drain out of Kelsey as she finally shook her head, evidently resigned to the inevitable. She touched a restraining hand to Lizzy's arm. "It's okay. I'll tell him. I should have told someone when this first started."

Lizzy stared at her. "Are you sure?"

"What difference does it make now?" But instead of looking at Jeb, she eased around in the chair until she could meet Dylan's gaze. "Paul wants drugs, prescription painkillers," she blurted in a rush. "He's addicted to them. He has been for a couple of years now."

"And that's why you left him?" Dylan guessed,

more relieved than shocked by the admission. Finally, they had something to work with.

"I left him because of that and because he was forging my name on prescriptions to get them. I agreed not to turn him in, if he would give me full custody of Bobby and stay out of our lives. I know that was wrong and probably stupid, but it was all I could think of to do at the time."

"And now his supply of pills has run out and he's desperate," Dylan concluded.

She nodded. "I'm sure that's it, even though he hasn't said as much. He wants me half-crazy, so I'll do whatever he says, give him whatever he wants."

Jeb whistled. "So we've got a guy who's hooked on drugs and not thinking rationally out there with your son."

"Jeb!" Dylan protested, seeing Kelsey's face turn a ghastly shade of gray at the harsh assessment.

"Sorry. My mouth runs ahead of my brain at times."

She waved off the apology. "I'm terrified of what he will do if he finds out I've told you all this. I promised to keep the secret."

"And he promised to stay away," Dylan said. "I'd say you're even." He hunkered down in front of her. "This helps, sweetheart. We have to assume he won't go far, because he's going to want to make a quick exchange for Bobby when the time comes. He may be moving from motel to motel, but I'll bet he's within a hundred miles or less."

"But you've checked all the motels over and over," Kelsey said. "He's not there."

"What about campgrounds?" Jeb suggested. "Are there any close by?"

"No," Lizzy said. "But there are acres and acres of open land. He could have pitched a tent anyplace."

Dylan exchanged a look with his brother. "Feel like taking a drive?"

Jeb nodded. "I've been dying to get a better look at this part of the country."

"I want to come with you," Kelsey said, half rising. Then her expression registered dismay and she sank back down. "But I can't, can I?"

"No," Dylan agreed. "You need to stay here in case he calls again. If he does, see if we're on track with this camping idea. Maybe you can get Bobby to say something about sleeping outdoors."

"Bobby hates bugs," she murmured. "If that's what they're doing, it's no wonder he was so cranky the last time we talked."

"I hate to burst your bubble, but I just remembered something. I thought Bobby said something about Paul not letting him leave the room," Lizzy said. "Doesn't that mean they have to be in a motel?"

"He did," Kelsey agreed. "Was that last time? Or the time before? I'm getting it all mixed up."

"It's okay," Dylan reassured her. "We'll take a look around anyway. Call me on the cell phone if anything comes up."

She nodded, then opened her mouth to say something, but fell silent, her expression guilty.

Dylan had a pretty good idea what she'd been about to say, though. He gave her a grin. "It's okay, darlin'. I know I'm fired. This one's on the house."

Chapter Nine

Dylan and Jeb were almost out the door when the phone rang. Everyone froze. Kelsey's heart began to thud dully as it had every time a call came in. She reached for the receiver with fingers that trembled so badly she could barely grasp it.

"Hello."

"Mommy?"

Bobby's voice sounded scratchy and hoarse. "Baby, are you okay? What's wrong?"

"Don't feel good, Mommy."

Kelsey had never felt so thoroughly helpless in her entire life. Maternal instinct as much as her professional training kicked in. Thank heaven Bobby was now old enough to answer a few simple questions. "Where does it hurt, sweetie? Your tummy? Your head?"

"All over. I'm hot, Mommy."

Her fury and frustration boiled over. "Put your daddy on the phone, baby. Okay?"

Paul came on the line. "He's fine," he said before she could get a word out. "It's just a little fever. It's no big deal, so don't go making a federal case out of it."

"I want him home, Paul. I'm the doctor. I'll be the judge of whether or not he's seriously ill."

"Kids get fevers. It's nothing," he insisted.

"Does he have a cold? Is that it? Have you been taking him in and out of air-conditioning?"

"Tsk-tsk," he chided. "You know I'm not going to answer something like that. Gotta run, Kelsey. Bobby wants some orange juice. I'll be in touch."

"Paul!" she shouted, but she could hear the click of his receiver being put back into place. "Dammit, Paul." This time the words came out as a frustrated whisper.

Her gaze sought out Lizzy, then automatically shifted to Dylan. It didn't seem to matter that she was furious at him for deceiving her about his own custody situation. She still looked to him for strength. How had that happened in such a short time? How did she know that despite everything, despite the angry accusations she had hurled at him, she could still trust him? With just a glance from her, he crossed the kitchen in three long strides. He pulled a chair up close beside her.

"Bobby's sick?" he asked.

"Paul says it's just a fever. Maybe he's right. He's probably right," she said more emphatically. "But I hate not being there, not knowing for sure."

"Of course you do," Lizzy said. "But stop a minute. Bobby's never had more than the sniffles. He's the healthiest little boy I've ever seen. There's no reason to imagine that this is anything more than that."

"Maybe he's overdue," Kelsey whispered, wishing she shared Lizzy's certainty. "Who knows where he's been the past few days or what he's been exposed to. He said he hurt all over."

"Could be the flu, then," Lizzy suggested, still maintaining a positive outlook. "It'll be over and done with in a day or so."

"Or it could be measles or chicken pox," Kelsey retorted, her imagination whirling into overdrive. She was suddenly thinking like a panic-stricken mom, rather than a cool, rational doctor. "We don't know. That's the problem."

Dylan gave a nod to Lizzy and Jeb, who vanished on cue. "Come here," he said, reaching for her.

Kelsey instinctively gravitated into his embrace, the previous night's argument forgotten. Dylan might not be able to cure whatever ailed Bobby, but she found comfort and reassurance in his touch. It was a reaction she didn't care to examine too closely.

"You heard what Lizzy said," he soothed. "Bobby's as healthy as a kid can be. This is probably nothing."

"But what if it's not?" she whispered.

"Then Paul will get medical attention for him."

She backed away. "Why on earth would you think that? He's not going to give up this game just to help Bobby, not until he gets what he wants from me."

"Then he'll make a demand. You'll give him the pills. And we'll get Bobby back. He won't risk that little boy's life. No father could do that, even if he's not thinking clearly."

"I wish I shared your faith," she said.

"You married the man, Kelsey. He can't be all bad. Wasn't there a time when you trusted him, when you had faith he would do the right thing?"

She thought back to the early days of their courtship, when Paul had been tender and funny and attentive. He had actually taken time off from work once to nurse her through a bad cold. So, Dylan was probably right. The man she had fallen in love with wouldn't let his son suffer.

"Thank you for reminding me of that," she said at last. "It's just that he changed so much after the pills."

"You hang on to the fact that he was a decent guy when you met him, okay?" He cupped her cheek in his hand. "A few prayers wouldn't hurt, either."

"I've prayed so often the last few days, I'm sure God is sick of hearing from me."

Dylan chuckled. "I don't think it works that way. I think He expects us to check in regularly with updates in circumstances like this."

Kelsey sighed and rested her forehead against Dylan's chest. She could feel the steady beating of his heart. "I was so nasty to you last night. Can you forgive me? I know you've been doing your best on this case. I had no right to accuse you of doing anything less."

Dylan sighed. "Yes, you did. The truth is I did come into this case with enough baggage to keep a shrink busy for a year. I never let it interfere, but it was there. And you had every right to know about it, to make a choice about whether you could trust me. I suppose I didn't want you to know for fear you'd dump me right at the beginning when time was critical. I knew right then that I was all you had to count on and that I'm damned good at what I do. My ego got in the way."

He tipped her chin up, then gazed directly into her eyes. "I'm with you a hundred percent on this, Kelsey. Okay?"

She nodded, unable to speak because she knew how terribly difficult it must be for him to side against a father who'd been cut off from his son, even under these extenuating circumstances.

"Dylan, will you talk to me about Shane?" She felt his muscles tense at the mention of his son's name. "Please? I'd like to hear about him."

"After this is all over, you and I will talk," he promised eventually. "About Shane and a good many other things, I imagine. Will that do?"

She was disappointed by the delay, but she nodded. "Yes. That will do."

"Then it's a date, darlin'. Now let me get out of here and catch up with Jeb. I'm not doing you a bit of good standing around here in your kitchen."

"Yes, you are," she said, but she stepped back just the same. "You're just not finding Bobby. And that's the only thing that matters now."

He bent down and pressed a hard kiss to her lips, then took off without another word. Kelsey watched him go, then sat down at the table and rested her head on her arms.

"Dear God," she whispered. "Make this the day that my son comes home to me. And in the meantime, please keep him and all the people looking for him safe."

"Amen," Lizzy said, adding her voice to Kelsey's.

Either her timing was impeccable or she had never strayed far from the kitchen and had heard Dylan leave. Kelsey looked up at her friend. "I am so incredibly lucky," she told her. "I have you and your family and this community to lean on."

"And Dylan," Lizzy reminded her.

A half smile formed. "And Dylan," she agreed. "He's an amazing man, isn't he?"

"Definitely one of the good guys." Lizzy searched her face intently. "Have you fallen for him, Kelsey?"

"I can't even think about something like that right now," she insisted, but in her heart she suspected that she was indeed falling in love with Dylan Delacourt. Finding out for sure was something that would have to wait until her son was safely home again.

Dylan drove himself to exhaustion that day and the next. He kept thinking of that little boy, his body flushed with fever, missing his mommy.

"I could wring the man's neck," he told Jeb.

"Which is why I'm here, to keep you from doing something stupid. We're going to find Bobby, take him home to Kelsey, and leave his daddy in one piece for the authorities to deal with.''

Dylan regarded his brother ruefully. ''Don't make me regret bringing you over here.''

Jeb laughed. ''You know I'm right. That's exactly why you brought me over here, to temper your hot head. I'm the cool, rational thinker, remember?''

''Since when?''

''Okay, compared to you, I am,'' Jeb amended.

''And you don't have the slightest urge to pummel Paul James's face to a bloody pulp?'' Dylan asked.

Jeb drew himself up and returned Dylan's skeptical look evenly. ''Absolutely not. Do I look like a thug?''

''No, you look like a man who's having the time of his life. When are you going to tell dear old Dad that you want to come to work with me full-time?''

Jeb's expression fell. ''On his deathbed, probably. The news will probably revive him just so he can make sure it doesn't happen.''

''Life's too short to waste it doing something you hate,'' Dylan said.

''I did talk to him about doing some corporate investigative work for him,'' Jeb revealed. ''He looked at me as if I'd suggested there were cockroaches in the pantry and I wanted to play at being an exterminator.''

''Is there something going on at the company that needs investigating?'' Dylan asked, startled by the suggestion that there might be. ''He hasn't mentioned anything.''

''Because he's in denial. You know Dad. He

thinks he's in total control of his universe. You were his first slipup. Then Trish's defection shook him badly. He's got the rest of us under tighter rein than ever. As for anyone stealing from him, to hear him tell it, it's impossible.''

''But you don't think so?''

''There are too many coincidences for my liking. Twice now, just when we were about to close a deal for a new site, another company has come in and snatched it out from under us.''

Dylan was stunned. He didn't believe in coincidences of that magnitude, either. He was surprised that his father did. ''Why isn't Dad acting on this?''

''Either he's in denial or he doesn't want to admit the obvious, that his new geologist is on the take.''

''Beautiful Brianna is selling corporate secrets?'' He thought he heard something else in his brother's voice, too. ''You're unhappy about more than the soured deals, aren't you? Is it Brianna?''

Jeb sighed. ''She's a terrific woman. I don't want to believe she's involved, but everything points to it.''

''Then forget Dad. Investigate on your own. Find out if she can be trusted.''

''What if my judgment's clouded by my hormones?''

''Believe me, Jeb, you won't be the first one. Look at me. Kelsey's got me tied up in knots. Besides, even though I know she was justified in going after full custody of Bobby, a part of me is still sympathetic to her ex. Of course, I've been getting over that in a hurry the last few days. I've finally concluded the man is pond scum and doesn't deserve so much as a glimpse of his son ever again.''

He spotted a diner up ahead and pulled into the lot. "I don't know about you, but I need coffee and some food. The last decent meal we had was that breakfast Trish cooked yesterday."

"And the cinnamon rolls Lizzy sent along," Jeb said.

"Cinnamon rolls? I never saw any cinnamon rolls."

"Oops. Sorry. I think what we both need is a good night's sleep," Jeb countered, quickly changing the subject. "We must have covered a thousand miles today, going in circles. I never knew so many sleazy motels existed."

"After we eat, if you want to go back to Trish's I'll drop you off. I want to check in at Kelsey's anyway."

"Sounds like a plan."

Dylan drank three cups of lousy coffee with his burger and fries. He figured that was enough caffeine to carry him through the night. Once he'd seen Kelsey, he was going out again. There was a better chance of spotting Paul's car at night. The man might stay on the run during the day, but surely he would stop to sleep.

He dropped Jeb off with a promise to pick him up again at daybreak, then headed for Kelsey's. It was already late, but the lights were still blazing and there were cars in the driveway, including the sheriff's. Dylan rang the bell. It was Justin who answered.

"Hey, Dylan, come on in. I was just filling Kelsey in on what we learned today."

"Which is?"

"We found Paul's car abandoned at the Dallas-Fort Worth airport."

Dylan muttered a harsh expletive. "He's taken off, then?"

Justin shook his head. "We don't think so. I put every man on it. They've checked every flight roster, every ticket counter in the airport. If Paul and Bobby were there, they were well disguised and traveling under assumed names."

Relief spread through Dylan. "Thank God. You figure they just dumped the car because he'd concluded by now that we might be trying to trace it?"

Justin nodded, then smiled. "And here's the best part. Either he's right there at the airport, in one of the hotels nearby, or he's managed to get his hands on a rental with a phony ID. We're getting close, pal. I can feel it."

"How's Kelsey taking it?"

"Like a trouper. She's mad enough to spit nails. If she didn't have to stay here in case Paul calls, I think she'd tear that airport area apart on her own."

"No need," Dylan said. "I'll do it for her. As soon as I talk to her, I'm on my way." He started for the living room, then turned back. "What if Paul bought an electronic ticket? Or bought the tickets in town? No one at a ticket counter would have seen him. Did you cover the people who work the gates?"

Justin muttered a curse. "We'll get on it now. I'll call the lead guy I have over there. I sent about ten volunteers to scour the place, along with one deputy. It was the best I could do without bringing in the Dallas area authorities. Kelsey's still opposed to that. Any idea why yet?''

Dylan nodded and explained about Paul and the pills. ''She made him a promise not to involve the police in the whole incident with the stolen prescription pads and forged prescriptions. She's been trying to stick to it, even though Paul has broken his part of their agreement.''

Justin muttered a curse. ''If his supply's running out, he could be increasingly unstable.''

''That's what I'm afraid of, too,'' Dylan agreed.

That said, he went on into the living room where a number of Adams wives had gathered to lend moral support. Most of their husbands were either involved in the search or were doing double duty at various ranches to cover for those who were out looking for Bobby.

Kelsey's gaze immediately shot to Dylan. ''You heard?''

Lizzy moved aside to make room for Dylan next to Kelsey on the sofa. He sat in the spot she'd vacated. ''Justin filled me in. I'm going to head for Dallas again in a little while.''

''Then you agree he's close to the airport?''

Dylan nodded.

''So he can leave in a hurry,'' she whispered, a catch in her voice as she searched for his expression for confirmation.

''Maybe just because it's a busy place with lots of strangers,'' he soothed. ''No one would notice him and Bobby there.''

"Bobby loves airplanes," she told him. "He's only flown a couple of times, but he stops whatever he's doing when one flies overhead and points to it. He'd be crazy about being at an airport or getting on a plane. He wouldn't think twice about it."

"Darlin', hold on a second. There's no reason to think he's gotten on a plane. Justin's been keeping a close eye on all the flight rosters. If Paul is near the airport now, it's happened very recently."

She stared at him, clearly surprised. "What makes you say that?"

"You've been listening for background noise whenever you talked to them, right? You didn't hear any planes when you talked to Bobby the other day, did you? Or any other time?"

"No," she said. Her expression slowly brightened as understanding dawned. "And if he'd been near the airport, I wouldn't have been able to miss the noise, would I?"

"I don't think so. Not as busy as DFW is." He studied her face, saw the deepening shadows under her eyes, the unmistakable exhaustion. "Why don't you try to catch a few hours of sleep?"

"We've all been telling her the same thing," Lizzy said. "She won't budge."

Dylan gave her a speculative look. "Is that so? I think I have a solution." He stood and scooped her up before she had a chance to react, then headed for the stairs. Their progress was greeted by amused looks from all the women.

"Dylan, put me down right this second," she demanded in a hushed tone. "You have no right. I am perfectly capable of deciding when I need to go to sleep.''

"Then do it," he said tersely, climbing the steps. He met her furious, indignant gaze. "Say it, Kelsey. You're the doctor. Admit you're beat and that you need some rest."

"I will not."

"Stubborn woman."

"Arrogant man."

He chuckled. "Now that we've established that, how about pointing out which room is yours?"

She frowned. "Why should I help you?"

He shrugged, shifted her more tightly against him, and poked his head in the room where he'd seen her the other night just to be sure it was Bobby's. "Must be the one down the hall," he concluded. He nudged open the door with his knee and stepped inside.

The room was the antithesis of what he'd expected. Kelsey was a coolly competent physician. Her home was neat as a pin, the furniture more practical than stylish. But the bedroom…oh, brother. There was no mistaking it was the room of a woman, a very sensuous woman. Dylan felt as out of place as he would have amid the lacy lingerie at Victoria's Secret. He also started getting a whole lot of ideas that had nothing to do with sleep.

The bed was king-sized and inviting. It was covered with a thick, floral-printed comforter in shades of rose and green, and piled high with pillows, some in satin cases, others trimmed with lace and velvet. A vase of white and pink roses in full bloom sat beside the bed, filling the air with their sweet scent. A slinky nightgown, made of some incredibly silky fabric that promised to reveal all sorts of fascinating secrets about the wearer, had been tossed on the bed.

On the dresser, there were at least a dozen fancy antique perfume bottles. Lipstick and other feminine secret weapons were scattered among them.

And on a table beside the bed, a radio had been left on and forgotten. It was tuned to a station that played ballads and love songs all day long.

Dylan was so taken with everything, so intrigued by what it revealed of the woman in his arms that he didn't move for fully a minute. For just as long he completely forgot about Bobby, the people downstairs and everything else.

"Dylan?" Kelsey finally whispered, a catch in her voice.

"Uh-huh?" He snapped back to reality, then moved to the bed and lowered Kelsey onto it. His gaze locked with hers.

"You know I want to stay right here with you," he said, his voice thick with longing. His body ached with arousal.

Eyes wide, she nodded. "I wish you could," she admitted, then covered her face. "Oh, God, what kind of woman does that make me? How can I even think such a thing while my son is missing?"

"You're just human, darlin'. So am I." He touched her cheek. "Rain check?"

"Yes," she said so softly he almost didn't hear her.

He shook off the feeling of being caught up in something that didn't make sense, something that was pulling at him and clouding his brain.

"Darlin', you sure do know how to motivate a

man.'' He winked at her. ''If there's a God in heaven, I'll have Bobby back here before morning.''

''As desperately as I want that,'' she said. ''It's enough just to know that you're trying. I know you'll find him for me, Dylan, however long it takes.''

Chapter Ten

Once he hit Dallas, Dylan knew he was racing against the clock. Paul wouldn't wait forever before making his demands. If this really was about pills and not about Bobby's custody, then sooner or later his need for the narcotics was going to outweigh whatever satisfaction he was getting from torturing Kelsey.

He took Jeb with him and together they scoured the airport, looking for anyone who might have caught a glimpse of Paul. Even though it was turf Justin's men had covered, Dylan wanted no stone left unturned.

He finally left Jeb sweet-talking ticket agents into checking their computers for reservations for a father and son, under any name at all. It was peak travel time and the airport was a madhouse, but if anyone could wheedle the information out of an employee, it was Jeb. He had the charm and the patience for it. Dylan was running out of both.

He went back to his car, which was stifling in the summer heat, turned the air-conditioning on full blast, then used his cell phone and called one of his contacts to do another check of Paul's credit-card records. Surely by now he was running low on cash. Maybe he'd finally slipped up and used plastic for something, *anything,* that would give them a lead. His using it to book a hotel room or a flight would, no doubt, be asking too much, but maybe he would have seen no harm in using it to pay for a meal or buy some T-shirts for Bobby.

While he waited for a call back, he studied the locator map he'd picked up in the airport. Hotels for the surrounding area were highlighted. He'd checked most of them just days ago, but with Paul's car turning up in the airport parking garage, maybe he'd taken a room in one of them since then.

"Dammit, where is he?" he muttered. He hated failing under any circumstances, but this was Kelsey's son they were talking about. Dylan would never forgive himself if the boy slipped through their fingers due to some oversight of his. He was as driven to succeed as he would have been if it had been Shane's fate at stake.

When his cell phone finally rang, he grabbed it.

"We've got a break," Frank Lane told him. "He used the credit card this morning."

"Where?"

"Don't get too excited. I'm not sure it'll help."

"Anything will help at this point."

"He used it at an airport gift shop."

"What for?"

"Coloring books and children's Tylenol."

Which meant that Bobby still had his fever, Dylan concluded. That wasn't good news. The toys were probably meant to distract a cranky child.

"Is there any way to tell which shop?"

"It took some doing," Frank said, "but the woman at the credit-card company was able to track it to the one closest to the Trans-National ticket counter."

"Thanks, pal. I owe you." He hung up, then called Jeb inside the terminal and relayed the information.

"Got it," Jeb said. "I'm on my way."

If Paul was buying tickets, toys and medicine inside the airport, he had to be staying close by. Dylan set off to recheck each of the hotels he'd visited a few days earlier.

He hit pay dirt at the fifth hotel. The desk clerk recognized Paul and Bobby from the pictures Dylan showed him.

"But you're out of luck," he said. "They checked out about an hour ago."

Dylan bit back a groan. "How'd the boy look? I heard he's been sick."

"A little pale and quiet, maybe, but he looked okay to me."

"The man didn't say where they were going?"

"No, just that he had a business meeting scheduled not far from here."

In Los Piños, no doubt, Dylan thought wearily.

Would he head straight there? Probably not. But he might pick a new hotel between here and there.

Working on the assumption that the shortest distance between two points was a straight line, Dylan went back to his car and headed southwest without waiting to hear from Jeb. He doubted his brother would learn anything critical from the gift shop and, if he did, he could reach him on his cell phone. It was more important that he start hitting every single hotel or motel along the highway. He figured he had twenty-four hours, maybe less, before this whole case was going to blow wide-open.

It was midmorning when Kelsey's cell phone rang. She was so startled by the sound coming from her purse that it took her a minute to make sense of it.

Suddenly the knot in her stomach tightened. Her gut told her it was Paul and that this time he intended to make all of his demands. He was using the cell phone for the first time because he'd assumed that by now her regular line would be tapped. She hadn't even thought to tell the police about this phone. Paul knew she kept it primarily for emergency use on the road or when the hospital needed to reach her. How could he be thinking so rationally, so diabolically, when she was all but incoherent from the stress?

Maybe it was for the best that she was alone for the first time in days, except for the sheriff's deputy outside. Maybe she could walk a verbal tightrope and reach an agreement with Paul knowing that there were no eavesdroppers to challenge her decision. She took a deep breath and answered the phone.

"Hiya, sweetheart," Paul greeted her, sounding as if they'd just parted days ago on friendly terms, as if they hadn't argued two endless days ago about Bobby's spiking fever.

"Paul, where the hell are you?" she asked, even though she knew better than to expect an answer. "How is Bobby? How's his fever?"

"Bobby's just fine. I told you he would be. He and I are having a blast, aren't we, little buddy?" he said with forced joviality.

Kelsey couldn't hear Bobby's response. "Let me talk to him," she demanded.

"I don't think so. Not this time."

"Now, Paul," she insisted. A terrible sensation of panic washed over her. What if Bobby couldn't talk? What if he was terribly ill and Paul was keeping it from her? "I want to hear for myself that his cold or whatever it was is better."

"Not until we get a few things straight," he countered.

Kelsey fought the longing to scream at him, to rant and rave until he gave in. Because, of course, he wouldn't give in, no matter how desperately she pleaded or how loudly she shouted. He would only hang up on her. She sensed that he was at the end of his rope. She had to make herself go along with him a little longer.

"Such as?" she asked finally.

"I need a supply of pills."

Hearing at long last what she had suspected from the beginning made her see red. "Is that what this is about, Paul? Is it really only about your addiction?''

"I'm not addicted. I'm in pain."

"Then see a doctor."

"Isn't that what I'm doing, doll?"

Frustration and fury brought stinging tears to her eyes. "How can you use Bobby this way?" she whispered. "He's your son. We made an agreement."

"And I wound up with nothing," he said bitterly.

"You stayed out of jail," she reminded him. "That should have been enough."

"It wasn't. I want more, Kelsey. I need those pills. It's not like I'm asking for an illegal substance."

"You might as well be," she countered.

"You're a doctor. You can prescribe them."

"Dammit, Paul, I can't do it. What you're asking, the quantities you want me to give you, it's illegal. I could lose my license."

"Not with all those powerful friends of yours. They'll see that you keep your practice. This is a one-time deal, Kelsey. Get me enough pills now and I'll never bother you again."

"Why should I believe that? When we signed our agreement, you said it was over, that you'd go into treatment. Yet here you are. And when this supply runs out, you'll be back again. Face it, there aren't enough pills in the world for a man who's addicted to them. You need help."

"And I'll get it. I promise," he said, a coaxing note in his voice. "Please, Kelsey. One last time."

She knew she would break eventually, that she

had to for Bobby's sake, but she forced herself to say no once more, steeling herself for another explosion.

"Not even for Bobby?" he asked, his voice suddenly cold. "Do this or you'll never see him again. I'm a whole lot better at running and hiding than you are. I have the resources. And I have less to lose."

"You'll never be able to work for a brokerage firm again," she reminded him, trying to keep a note of desperation out of her voice.

"With my investments, I won't have to."

Dear God, she knew it was true. He'd made a fortune for his clients and, in the process, for himself. He would take her boy just for spite and she would never see him again. She would be dooming her son to a life on the run with a father who cared more for his next fix than for him. She had tried to prepare herself for this moment, tried to accept that he'd left her no choice, but it still made her feel sick.

"What do you want?" she said, resigned.

"Pills, painkillers to be precise, and lots of them."

"They're regulated. I can't just write a prescription for hundreds of them at once."

"You figure out how to do it, sweetheart. Just have them for me by this time tomorrow or Bobby and I will disappear."

"Where should I bring them?"

"I'll be in touch."

He hung up before she could ask anything more, before she could demand one more time to hear her baby's voice. Trembling violently, she forced herself to walk outside. She found the deputy on the porch.

"My husband called," she said in an emotionless voice. "He wants pills and he wants me to have them ready by tomorrow."

He regarded her sympathetically. "Yes, ma'am. Are you okay?"

"I'll be fine," she said, but her knees buckled and she sank into a rocker, still clutching the cell phone.

"I'll call Sheriff Adams right away, Dr. James. It won't take a minute for him to get here."

She nodded, then realized Justin wasn't the person she desperately needed right now. She needed Dylan. With shaking fingers she managed to punch in the number she'd memorized, then waited for him to answer his cell phone.

"Delacourt."

"Dylan…" Her voice trailed off.

"Kelsey, what's happened?"

"Paul called. He wants me to have a lot of pills ready for him tomorrow. He said he'd call back about a meeting place. I have to do it. I don't have a choice."

"Does Justin know?"

"The deputy just went to radio him. He should be here in a few minutes."

"Good," he said. "Okay, here's what I think you should do. Can you come up with placebos that look enough like whatever he wants?"

Her spirits lifted at the obvious solution. "Of course," she said, suddenly feeling confident that she could handle this without just turning over a satchel full of narcotics to her ex-husband.

"Then that's what you'll do. Call Sharon Lynn to see if Dolan's has what you need. Otherwise, call the Garden City Hospital pharmacy. Justin can go and pick up the supply so we'll be ready whenever Paul calls back. He can make it all nice and legal so you won't have problems later."

"What are you going to do? Will you come back?"

"Not just yet. I'm heading that way, but I want to finish checking the hotels and motels between the Dallas airport and Los Piños. He's got to be close enough to get to you and then get out of here in a hurry. I'd like to find him before he sets up the meeting, but if not we'll get him then, Kelsey. Just hang on a little longer and you'll have your son back."

She was suddenly struck by a terrible thought. "Dylan, what if…?" She couldn't even bring herself to voice her greatest fear.

"What if…?" he prodded. "What's worrying you?"

"That he'll come without Bobby."

"I don't think he'll try that. There won't be any incentive for you to give him what he wants, if he doesn't have Bobby with him."

"He'll just take the pills. He's a strong man. He keeps himself in shape. I might not have a choice."

"It will be fine. You'll have backup, if it comes to that."

"What do you mean, 'if it comes to that'?"

"I intend to find him first," he said tersely.

"Thank you," she whispered. "I know I need to let you get back to work, but I feel stronger just hearing the sound of your voice. Thank you for sticking with this even after I fired you.''

He chuckled lightly. ''Did you fire me? I don't seem to remember that.''

''When this is over, I'm going to make it up to you,'' she promised.

''I'll hold you to that, doc.''

A few minutes later, when Justin arrived, Kelsey was feeling calmer. She'd already made a note of the type of placebos that she thought would fool Paul, at least long enough that she would be able to grab Bobby away from him. She'd checked with Sharon Lynn. Dolan's had some in stock and Sharon Lynn was already making arrangements with the hospital pharmacy in Garden City for more.

''I want to make the exchange,'' she told Justin. ''I want Bobby in my arms before Paul gets these pills and has time to find out they're fakes. Otherwise, if he figures out I've tricked him, he'll take Bobby and vanish.''

''I think you should leave it to a professional,'' Justin argued.

''He's not going to deal with a professional,'' Kelsey countered. ''He's only going to want to deal with me, anyway, and you know it. I have to be ready, Justin. You might as well help me figure out what to do.''

Justin looked as if he wanted to argue, but wisely he didn't. ''Why don't we just wait and hear what his demands for the meeting are?''

''Fine,'' Kelsey said, gathering strength and resolve. ''But I have a few demands of my own this time and, by God, he'd better be ready to agree to them.''

The next few hours were endless. Justin kept the neighbors and his family away, except for Lizzy, but not even her best friend could keep Kelsey from growing more frantic with every second that passed. Sharon Lynn brought the pills by in a duffel bag.

"Do you think that's enough?" she asked worriedly. "It's not exactly like stuffing a bag with cash. Even though there are a lot of them, they don't take up much space."

Kelsey glanced in the bag and saw at least two dozen large, unlabeled prescription bottles, each of which probably held two hundred tablets. Had these been the real thing, anyone using them as a legitimate doctor prescribed could go for years on what was in the bag. For someone addicted like Paul, it was impossible to say what his reaction would be.

"It will have to be enough," Kelsey said grimly. "I'll tell him it was all I could get on short notice. It's not like a town this size has a major drug company around the corner. I'll tell him if he wants more, he'll have to wait until you can get another shipment in. He won't want to do that."

Sharon Lynn wrapped her in a tight hug. "I'm so sorry you're going through this. I look at my own two kids and try to imagine how I'd feel…" She shuddered. "It was awful enough when I thought I was going to lose my daughter to that horrible biological grandmother of hers. I can't even think about something like this."

"Hopefully, you'll never have to face anything like it," Kelsey said. She patted the bag. "Thank you for these. I'll pay you for them after all this is over.''

"You'll do nothing of the kind," Sharon Lynn said fiercely. "We look out for our own around here and you're one of us. Besides, if the police take Paul into custody, these won't be gone long."

"But they'll be evidence. You won't be able to put them back in stock," Kelsey protested.

"It doesn't matter," Sharon Lynn insisted.

Tears stung Kelsey's eyes. She tried to blink them back, but couldn't. Instead, she turned and walked away. Lizzy moved beside her and silently handed her a tissue.

"Tell Sharon Lynn I'm sorry," she whispered, her voice choked. "It's just that everyone is being so kind."

"There's no need to be sorry, not with any of us," Lizzy said. "Why don't you just have a good cry and get it out of your system?"

"I can't fall apart now," Kelsey said, drawing in a deep breath and trying to pull herself together as Sharon Lynn came to join them. "This is it. I have to be ready."

"I think you're the strongest woman I've ever met," Lizzy told her.

"Not me. I'm just trying to survive a nightmare."

"Sometimes surviving takes more strength than anything else," Sharon Lynn chimed in softly. "After Kyle died in that accident on our wedding night, I thought I wouldn't make it, but I did. Then Cord and my baby came into my life and everything changed. I'm living proof that you can survive anything."

Kelsey clung to that as the hours dragged on. There was no word from Dylan either. Kelsey had resigned herself to the fact that there would be no last-minute rescue. By the time the cell phone finally rang after midnight, she knew she was going to have to deal with Paul directly.

"Have you got them?" he asked without preamble.

"Yes," she said. "They're right here."

"Then we'll meet in the morning just after daybreak, six o'clock."

"Where?"

He described a place in the middle of nowhere, about halfway between Los Piños and Garden City. "There won't be anywhere for the cops to hide behind the bushes, so tell them to stay away," he warned.

"You're bringing Bobby, though, right?"

"No, but I'll tell you where to find him afterward."

"Forget it," she said vehemently. "I want to see Bobby. I want him with me before you get your hands on the pills."

"Don't you trust me, sweetheart?" he asked, sounding amused.

"Not as far as I could throw you."

"Well, that's too bad, because you're going to have to."

"Then you can forget all about your pills, Paul. I won't even bother showing up. Your decision."

She braced herself for an explosion. Her words hung in the air, leaving them stalemated. Silence fell. It went on for so long that she feared she'd overplayed her hand. But desperation for the pills finally won out.

"Okay, I'll bring him," he said at last. "But if you betray me, Kelsey, if the cops show up, I'll shoot you both and then I'll kill myself. No one will be able to save either one of you."

A chill ran down her spine at his words, not just because of the threat itself, but because of the I-have-nothing-to-lose way in which he said it. She knew then with a terrible sense of dread that any remnants of the decent man she'd once loved and married were gone, lost to the drugs that now tragically ruled his life.

Chapter Eleven

Dylan finally caught a break just before dawn at a sleazy motel on the northern outskirts of Garden City. The grizzled proprietor of the place looked like something out of an old Western. He wasn't especially pleased to have someone banging on his door in the middle of the night, which probably explained his cantankerous attitude.

Dylan noticed he didn't seem to have much interest in upkeep or in attracting business. He valued his guests' privacy so much, he didn't bother with a register or credit cards, either. But for the fifty bucks Dylan waved in front of him, he was eager enough to talk about the guests in room eight.

"Been here since late yesterday afternoon," he told Dylan. "Cute kid. Keeps crying for his mama, though. That father of his doesn't have much patience for it, either. I've heard him yelling at the boy to shut up.''

Dylan saw red. ''You didn't go down and check it out?''

The man shrugged. ''None of my business.''

Dylan bit back an angry retort. ''Are they there now?''

''What do you think? It's early. I suppose they're asleep like everyone ought to be, if you catch my meaning.''

Dylan ignored the sarcasm. ''But you don't know for sure?''

''Do I look like the nosy type?'' the old man retorted. ''People come and go. It's none of my concern, as long as the room's paid up.''

''If anything has happened to that boy, if there's so much as a bruise on him, it'll become your concern in a hurry,'' Dylan told him tightly. ''Now give me a key.''

''Can't do that,'' the man replied.

Dylan reached across the counter and grabbed a fistful of the man's hastily donned and still unbuttoned shirt. ''Give me a key or I'll knock down the damned door.'' He got the key. ''What kind of a car was the man driving?'' he asked.

''Something flashy. Surprised me that a man with a car like that would stay in a dump like this.''

Dylan walked to room eight, surveying the parking lot as he went. There were only a handful of cars parked outside the rooms and none could be described as flashy.

Outside room eight, Dylan listened at the door. He thought he heard the sounds of the television and maybe something else, possibly a child's whimpers. Just as he was about to open the door, a dark green sports car skidded into the spot in front of the room and a man he recognized at once as Paul James leapt out.

"Who the hell are you?" he demanded.

"A friend of Kelsey's," Dylan said, keeping his voice down. "I've come for Bobby."

"Like hell," Paul said, taking a swing at him. "Kelsey and I have a deal."

"I just changed it," Dylan countered.

To emphasize the point, Dylan's fist landed in Paul's pretty face. To his disappointment, the man sank to the ground like a stone. He'd been hoping to get in a few more punches. He stepped over him, opened the door and went inside. Bobby was huddled on the floor in front of the TV, clutching a stuffed bear, tears streaming down his flushed cheeks.

Dylan forced himself to stay calm and quiet, when he wanted badly to grab the boy up and hug him. He hunkered down. "Hey, Bobby."

"Who're you?" Bobby asked, regarding him suspiciously. "I heard you. You were fighting with my daddy. Where is he?"

"He's right outside. He'll be here in a few minutes." He was tempted to touch Bobby's forehead to see if he was as feverish as he looked, but he didn't dare. The boy was upset enough. Dylan wondered how long he'd been left here alone.

"How are you feeling?" he asked instead.

Bobby shrugged.

"Got a fever, maybe?"

"I guess," he said and inched backward.

"It's okay," Dylan soothed. "I'm not here to hurt you. Your mom sent me."

The boy's eyes went wide. "You know Mommy?"

"I sure do."

He uttered a tiny sigh and looked nervously toward the door. "Don't tell my daddy, but I miss Mommy."

Dylan grinned. "Want to talk to her? She'll tell you it's okay to come with me, all right?"

Bobby nodded eagerly.

Dylan took out his cell phone and placed the call to Kelsey.

"Paul?" she demanded, after snatching it up on the first ring.

"No, it's me, darlin'. I have someone here who'd like to speak to you." He handed the phone to Bobby.

"Mommy?" the boy said tentatively. At the sound of his mother's voice, his little face brightened. "Mommy!"

Dylan heard Kelsey's voice catch on a sob, then more of Bobby's excited chatter. He found himself blinking back tears. He gave the two of them another minute to talk, then said, "Hey, sport, let me talk to her, okay?"

Bobby reluctantly handed him the phone.

"Kelsey?"

"Oh, Dylan, where are you? Is he really okay? I was supposed to meet them in an hour on that old road west of Los Piños. When the phone rang, I thought it was Paul calling to cancel or change the meeting place. Where is he? Had he left Bobby behind?''

''No. He's right outside the room. I decked him on the way in.''

''Oh, God,'' she murmured, suddenly sounding panic-stricken. ''Dylan, did you check for a gun?''

''A gun?''

''He told me if I showed up with the police he would shoot me, Bobby and then himself. He has to have a gun.''

''Well hell,'' Dylan cursed, just in time to look up and straight into the barrel of the very gun in question.

''I'll take the phone now,'' Paul said with surprising calm for a man on drugs who'd just been leveled by a punch. His glass jaw didn't seem to be affecting his ability to aim straight.

Keeping one eye on Bobby, Dylan gave Paul the phone. He couldn't risk a confrontation with an armed man as long as Bobby was in range, not after the threat Paul had already made to kill Kelsey, his boy and himself if the police interfered.

''So, Kelsey, I guess you've heard there's been a new wrinkle,'' Paul said with what almost sounded like good cheer.

Dylan stared at him. Paul was enjoying this, which could only mean he was in a drug-induced fantasyland.

''This means we'll have a little change in plans. I think I'll bring your friend along with me, instead of Bobby. What's he worth to you?''

''Nothing,'' Dylan said, interrupting. ''I barely

even know your ex-wife. I'm just an investigator on the case. Nothing more.''

Paul looked skeptical. ''He says you don't give a damn about him, which could mean he'd be a lousy bargaining chip. What do you say?''

Dylan couldn't hear what Kelsey replied, but Paul's expression turned grim. ''I'm not bringing them both. You choose, Kelsey. Your pal here or Bobby.''

''She'll take Bobby,'' Dylan insisted, not giving her time to answer. ''Take her son back to her.''

Paul displayed a chilling smile. ''Why, aren't you the gallant gentleman? Just her type. Okay, Bobby goes. But what do I do with you?'' he wondered aloud. Then he raised his gun toward the ceiling and pulled the trigger.

Dylan heard Kelsey's scream just before Paul disconnected the phone.

''That ought to keep her focused on what's important,'' Paul said.

He motioned Dylan into the bathroom, removed his belt, then used it to bind Dylan's wrists and tie them securely to the shower rod. Satisfied that Dylan was immobilized, Paul went back into the room long enough to grab a tie, then added that to the belt to further restrain him.

''That ought to keep you out of action long enough for me to settle things with Kelsey and be on my way,'' Paul said. ''It ought to give her a few bad moments wondering if you're dead or not, too.''

''You really are a heartless son of a bitch,'' Dylan declared.

Paul didn't seem particularly distraught by the

characterization. It did, however, serve to remind him that once he was gone there was nothing to prevent Dylan from screaming for help. He found a handkerchief, stuffed it in Dylan's mouth, then used another tie to keep it in place.

"Daddy?" Bobby asked hesitantly, his eyes wide with fear. "Why are you hurting him? He's Mommy's friend."

"He's not hurt," Paul assured him. "Just out of commission for a bit."

Dylan winked at Bobby, hoping to relieve the boy's concern. Bobby had already been through enough. Besides, if he accepted that Dylan was okay, maybe he could pass the word on that along to Kelsey, who was already frantic enough without worrying about what had happened to him because he hadn't used his brain when he'd taken Paul down outside.

"Come on, son. Let's go see your mother."

Casting one last worried look over his shoulder, Bobby eventually followed his dad.

And Dylan got to work on freeing himself.

Kelsey stood holding the phone in her hand, aware that the blood had probably drained from her face.

"Oh, God, oh, God, oh, God." She kept murmuring it over and over.

Justin's firm grip on her shoulders finally caught her attention. She stared at him blankly. His mouth was moving, but she couldn't seem to grasp what he was saying.

"What, Kelsey? What happened?" He shook her gently. "Tell me."

"He shot Dylan. I was talking to Dylan and then Paul came in and took the phone and then he shot him." She stared at Justin guiltily. "It's all my fault. If he's dead, it's because of me."

"We don't know he's dead," Justin insisted. "Stop thinking like that."

"But he shot him," she repeated, not just sick to her stomach, but sick at heart.

"Dylan can take care of himself," Justin assured her. "Let's try to concentrate, okay? Can you do that? Is the meeting still on?"

Kelsey nodded. Her baby. She had to focus on getting her baby back. If she thought about Dylan, she would go crazy.

"Then let's go."

"No," she retorted fiercely. "Just me. I have to go alone. If he sees you there, he'll kill me and Bobby." She shuddered as she heard the terrible sound of that gun echoing in her head. She wondered if she would ever be able to shut it off. "He'll use the gun again. I know it."

"All the more reason for us to be there," Justin insisted. "I can have a sharpshooter standing by. Paul won't get a chance to use the gun, Kelsey. It has to be that way. He's out of control."

She knew Justin was right. Going to meet Paul alone was foolhardy. Her best chance to get Bobby back and to live was to have professional backup, but she was so scared that Paul would see them, that he would panic.

"I need your promise that you won't let him spot

you,'' she said, knowing how futile extracting such a promise was.

"We'll do our best,'' he vowed. "Nobody wants everybody to walk away from this safely more than I do. The last thing I want is Grandpa Harlan on my back if there's a screwup.''

The mention of his grandfather's reaction had the desired result. Kelsey found she could still smile. A moment ago she'd been so certain she would never smile or laugh again.

She drew in a deep breath and squeezed Justin's hand. "Then, by all means, let's not screw up,'' she said staunchly.

Paul's restraints were downright pitiful. All it took was a couple of quick, sharp tugs for Dylan to bring the shower rod crashing down. He slid belt and tie over the end and off. That loosened them enough for him to work his hands completely free. He was already racing from the room as he slipped the second tie over his head and jerked the wadded-up handkerchief from his mouth.

The sound of the gunshot and the shower rod crashing had stirred enough of the other guests to bring a small crowd into the parking lot.

"Which way did they go?'' Dylan shouted. "The man and the little boy? Which way did they turn?''

The proprietor ignored him and rushed toward the room. He gasped when he spotted the bullet hole. "Somebody's going to have to pay for the damage.''

"Take it out of the fifty I already gave you,'' Dylan snapped. He turned to one of the guests who looked wide-awake, but not especially terrified. "Did you see which way they turned?"

"West," the man said. "Should we call the police?"

"I'll do it," Dylan said. Of course, it wouldn't be the local police he'd be calling, but Justin. He punched in the number of his cell phone as he turned onto the highway.

"Sheriff's Department," Becky responded.

"Becky, it's Dylan. Can you get Justin for me?"

"He's on the road. I can't patch you through, but I can get him on the radio and relay messages," she said.

Dylan was impressed with the fact that she wasted no time. Clearly she grasped that Dylan wasn't calling just to chat. When she added, "I heard you were shot," he understood why.

"Not me," he corrected, "but the ceiling took a hit."

"Bad aim?"

"Nope, deliberate torture for Kelsey."

"What a creep!" she murmured, then said, "Okay, Dylan, I've got Justin. What do you want me to tell him?"

Dylan described his location and the car Paul was driving. "He's headed west toward the meeting place. He has Bobby and he has a gun. I'm maybe ten minutes behind him. Depending on how fast he's driving, I may catch up."

"Ten-four," Becky said briskly, then repeated the information to Justin. "Dylan, he wants you to stay clear. He has plenty of men to handle it. They're already in place. Back off. Do you read me?"

Dylan read her loud and clear, but he created the sound of static on the line, then deliberately hung up. There was no way in hell he was staying out of this now. It had gotten personal back there in that motel room.

Besides, he'd promised Kelsey that he would deliver Bobby safe and sound and he intended to do just that. This maverick streak of his had kept him from becoming a cop. But he also had sense enough to know what he could handle and what he couldn't. He could handle Paul James, especially now that he'd learned the hard way not turn his back on him. He accelerated and kept his gaze fixed intently on the highway ahead of him.

There was a turnoff about eight miles ahead that would head toward Los Piños. He guessed from Kelsey's earlier remark that the meeting point was about five miles beyond the turn. That gave him thirteen miles—or about ten minutes at seventy miles an hour—to catch Paul. After that, Kelsey was going to have to face her ex-husband. Dylan wanted to prevent that from happening if he possibly could.

He kept hearing her scream when she'd thought Paul had shot him. She had sounded genuinely anguished. That meant she'd be going into the meeting terrified or angry or both, when what was needed was a clear, cool head.

He pushed the car's speed up to eighty. Not ten seconds later he spotted the taillights of the flashy green car up ahead. At the same time, he saw a sheriff's car slide onto the highway from its hiding place behind a stand of trees. The cop didn't use lights or his siren, but there was no mistaking his intention to get Dylan off the road.

If Paul spotted that police car in his rearview mirror, there was no telling what he would do. It wouldn't matter that the deputy was after Dylan, not him. He could panic just the same, and that would increase the danger to Bobby and Kelsey.

Dylan knew he had no choice. Slamming his palm against the steering wheel in frustration, he muttered a curse and pulled to the side of the road. The deputy coasted to the shoulder right behind him, then exited his car slowly and strolled up to Dylan.

"You're in a mighty big hurry for this early in the morning," he noted.

Dylan flipped open his investigator's license. "I was tailing a suspect. Thanks to you, he's getting away."

The deputy didn't seem particularly distressed by the predicament he'd caused. "Is that so?" He studied Dylan intently. "That wouldn't be the same suspect that half the cops in West Texas are waiting for just up the road, now would it?"

Dylan grimaced. This little speed trap had been Justin's doing. He could feel it. The man was sneakier than Dylan had imagined. "It would indeed," he conceded.

The man nodded, then handed him back his wallet. "It's damned frustrating sitting around and letting somebody else take down the bad guys, isn't it?" he asked sympathetically.

"If you understand that, why'd you stop me?"

"Because *you* were the bad guy I was assigned

to take down,'' the deputy said. ''Want some coffee?''

Dylan gave a sigh of resignation. ''Might as well.''

The man gestured toward his cruiser. ''I've got a whole Thermos full right back there. Join me and we'll wait for news.''

''You go ahead,'' Dylan suggested. ''I'll be right there.''

The man raised his sunglasses and peered intently into Dylan's eyes. ''Son, what kind of fool do you take me for? The second I walk away, you'll take off like a bat out of hell.'' He gestured. ''Out of the car. And hand over your keys while you're at it.''

As badly as he wanted to do otherwise, Dylan got out of the car and gave the deputy his keys. He'd never catch Paul before he reached the meeting spot, anyway. It looked as if he was going to have to trust Justin to keep Kelsey and Bobby safe. Given how he'd sidelined Dylan, Justin was clever enough to handle the job.

And if he failed, Dylan would wring his neck. Though the prospect of doing bodily harm to the sheriff cheered him considerably, he found himself praying that there would be no reason for it. He'd rather find Kelsey and Bobby all in one piece when this was over.

The deputy regarded him sympathetically as he handed him a cup of coffee strong enough to wake the dead.

''Waiting's a bitch, isn't it?''

Dylan nodded. ''You got that right.''

* * *

Paul had spotted the car racing up behind him on the highway and knew in his gut it had to be the man he'd left tied up back at the motel. Dylan. That was his name. A friend of Kelsey's.

How had he gotten loose so quickly? Obviously Paul wasn't exactly equipped for a life of crime. Despite what they all thought, he didn't have a killer's instincts. Thankfully, today would be the end of it. Kelsey would give him the pills he needed and he would go back to Miami, where he belonged. He'd be back at work next week and this whole thing would be a distant memory.

"Daddy?"

He glanced down at Bobby and saw the fear in the boy's eyes. Guilt crept through him. He hadn't meant to scare his son. There'd been a time when Bobby had been his pride and joy, ranking right up there with Kelsey as two of the best things to ever happen to him.

He blamed the doctors for destroying all that. They were the ones who'd put him on such powerful narcotics after his skiing accident. Why couldn't Kelsey see it wasn't his fault he'd gotten hooked? Why had she blamed him when he hadn't been able to give them up? What kind of wife walked away from her husband when he was in trouble?

Once again the familiar anger swelled in his chest, crowding out the guilt. Still, he kept his tone even when he answered Bobby.

"Isn't this a blast, little buddy?"

Bobby's chin rose with a touch of defiance. He looked so much like Kelsey then, it was scary. "No,

Daddy. You're driving too fast. I don't like it. Driving fast is wrong.''

"Not out here in the country," Paul told him. "Out here it's okay to drive like the wind."

"No, it's not. Mommy said."

"Well, your mom's wrong about this one. Now, be quiet so Daddy can concentrate."

He glanced once again into his rearview mirror and saw that the car was gaining on him. It was no longer a distant dot on the horizon. He could see the front end well enough to tell the color and make. It was definitely the same one he'd seen in the motel parking lot, close to the office.

Suddenly a sheriff's cruiser slid onto the highway in hot pursuit. Paul felt a momentary flash of panic, then amusement as he realized the deputy was after the other man. He laughed when he saw the two cars pulling onto the shoulder of the highway, then fading into the distance as his own speed steadily accelerated.

Damn, he was good. It was about time he caught a break. Another hour, two at the outside, and he would be on his way home. This miserable Texas wasteland would be nothing but a distant memory.

Chapter Twelve

The air was hot and dry even though the sun was barely up. Kelsey sat in the car with the windows open just the same, listening desperately for the sound of an approaching vehicle. This road wasn't well traveled, which was precisely why Paul had chosen it. If she'd heard anything, more than likely it would be her ex-husband.

Would he have Bobby with him as he'd promised? Or had everything changed back at the motel? Had he actually shot Dylan and left him to die? She couldn't imagine Paul being that desperate and out of control, but there had been no mistaking the sound of that gunshot, the sudden silence as the phone had gone dead in her hand. Her stomach rolled over just thinking about it.

For the thousandth time, she prayed that Dylan

was still alive, that they would have a chance to explore the feelings that had begun to grow between them in the midst of this ordeal.

Later, she told herself firmly. She would think of that later. Right now, all that mattered was getting Bobby back. She tried to recall everything Justin had told her to do. She nearly panicked when the details wouldn't come, then simply prayed that any second now she would see her son again, that the nightmare would end.

She glanced surreptitiously toward the distant grove of trees where one of Justin's men waited, a sharpshooter designated to take Paul out, but only if something went awry. She'd had to beg for that much. She hadn't wanted Bobby to live with the horror of seeing his father shot, not if there was any other way to bring Paul into custody. If she'd had her choice, Paul wouldn't even be arrested where Bobby could witness it. Justin, however, had only been willing to bend his rules so far.

There were more men posted along the highway in both directions, wherever the slightest cover allowed them to remain hidden from view. They would not prevent Paul from coming in, but they were there to set up instantaneous roadblocks that would keep him from getting away.

Concentrate, she told herself. Stay calm. She glanced at the picture of Bobby she had clutched in her hand. That precious smile. Those laughing eyes. Just remember what's important, she instructed herself. She had to keep reminding herself that rescuing Bobby was paramount. There were others who could deal with Paul. Her time to lash out at him would come later, once her son was safe.

Straining her ears, she thought she detected the distant sound of an engine. Squinting into the sun, which had just crept above the horizon in a blaze of orange, she kept her gaze pinned on the highway, looking for the first flash of sun on chrome or a swirl of dust that would prove her ears hadn't deceived her.

"Come on. Come on," she murmured.

"Kelsey?"

The sound of Justin's voice crackling from the radio on the seat beside her made her pulse leap wildly. She grabbed it and whispered, "Yes," as if whoever was coming might hear her if she spoke any louder.

"This is it. We've spotted him. You doing okay?"

"I'm fine," she said with a certainty she was far from feeling. She *would* be fine, too, as soon as she saw her son, as soon as she held him.

She glanced toward the duffel bag filled with pills to reassure herself that her bargaining chip was in place.

"Don't do anything crazy," Justin warned her. "Remember, we're right here. Get Bobby. Give Paul the pills. Leave the heroics to us, okay?"

"Yes," she said, disgusted with herself because her voice squeaked instead of remaining steady.

"You'll do just fine," he reassured her. "Kelsey, one last thing."

Something more to remember? She wasn't sure

she could. "What?" she asked as she finally spotted the first glimpse of the car in the distance.

"Dylan's fine. I've talked to him and he's fine. Okay? I just thought you ought to know that before this goes down."

A terrible knot of tension in her stomach dissolved at the news. She knew why he'd told her, too. He hadn't wanted Paul to be able to use Dylan's so-called death to rattle her. He could have, too. If Paul had taunted her with the fact that Dylan was dead, she very well might have lost it and done something stupid.

"Thank God," she murmured.

"Okay, angel, let's do this," Justin said with the absolute calm of a professional. "You with me?"

Her nerves steadied, along with her resolve. "You bet," she said firmly.

"Everybody else?" Justin asked.

Kelsey was dimly aware of other deputies responding, then Justin's call for radio silence from here on out.

She sucked in a deep breath, then stepped from the car to wait for her ex-husband.

Dylan was chafing at the restrictions he was under. He'd listened to Justin's radio contact with Kelsey, heard the thread of fear in her voice, then the determination. She had to be the bravest woman he'd ever known.

He'd been relieved when Justin had told her that Paul hadn't left him for dead. He didn't want her thinking about anything except Bobby. He knew all too well how many things could go wrong when a person was even the tiniest bit distracted. That was how he'd ended up at Paul's mercy back at the motel.

The deputy glanced over at him. "She'll be fine. She sounds like a woman who can handle herself in a crisis."

"Give her a sick kid and she can, but this?" Dylan shrugged. "Can any parent ever be prepared to deal with something like this?"

Sitting here, waiting, was giving him way too much time to think—about Kelsey, about Bobby, about Kit, and about Shane. The first thing he intended to do when this ended was to see his son. To hell with the noble, decent decision he'd made. He wanted his boy to know he had a father who loved him. He didn't intend to disrupt their lives. He just wanted a chance to spend a few hours with Shane from time to time. He and Kit could work it out. He'd matured since the divorce. In the last few days, he'd learned he wasn't too old to learn to compromise when it really mattered.

An image of Bobby popped into his head. He couldn't help thinking about the future, making the inevitable comparison between any relationship he might have with Kelsey's son and the bond Kit's husband had formed with Shane. How would he feel if Paul James fought to remain a part of Bobby's life? Of course, he thought wryly, under the circumstances, it could be a very long time before Paul had any contact whatsoever with his son again.

Dammit, what was happening? The radio silence was setting his nerves on edge. Unconsciously, he leaned forward to listen, hoping for some clue about what was taking place just a few miles down the road.

"Do the right thing," he muttered as if Paul might somehow hear him.

"Now there's a prayer worth repeating," the deputy observed.

Dylan glanced at him and saw that his expression was tense, his frustration just as evident. Dylan's own resentment at being kept out of the heart of the action eased a little. He had a hunch with very little encouragement the deputy might be persuaded to creep a little closer.

He was even more certain that it was absolutely the wrong thing to do. So much as a whisper of activity might spook Paul. Dylan had seen for himself the shape the other man was in. It wouldn't take much for him to spin out of control.

"You figure Justin has things under control up there?" Dylan asked, half looking for an excuse to change his mind.

"As much as any man could under the circumstances," the deputy responded.

"Then I guess we'll do what he intended us to do. Sit tight."

"Got to say it's not in my nature," the man said.

"Mine, either," Dylan said with heartfelt agreement.

Even so, they sat and waited.

Paul's car eased to a stop about ten feet behind Kelsey's. The passenger door opened at once and Bobby emerged with a whoop of excitement.

"Mommy!" he called and ran toward her, even as Paul was shouting at him to stop.

Kelsey and Bobby both ignored him. She knelt down and opened her arms, tears streaking down her cheeks. At the feel of his warm, solid little body next to hers, she trembled violently. A relief unlike anything she had ever felt before washed over her. It was several minutes later, with Bobby squirming to get free, before she released him, then rocked back on her heels to study him.

Bobby stared at her, his expression puzzled. "Mommy, why are you crying?"

"I'm just glad to see you, that's all. I've missed you."

"I missed you, too."

She ran a hand over his cheek, then touched his forehead to reassure herself that his fever was truly gone.

"Mommy," Bobby protested, wriggling away from the touch.

"I guess you don't need any of Mommy's kisses to make you better, after all," she said.

"I told you he was fine," Paul said.

The sound of his voice startled her. How had she forgotten about him? He was the reason they were out here. Controlling the surge of anger that rushed through her, she stood slowly and met his gaze.

She forced herself not to flinch when she saw the wild look in his eyes. "Thank you for bringing him back to me," she said, knowing that it could easily have gone another way.

"I told you I would. Now you need to keep your end of the bargain."

"The pills are in the car."

"You get them for me."

She didn't bother arguing. But as she moved toward the car, she took Bobby's hand. "Come on, sweetie. Help me get the bag I brought for Daddy."

"No," Paul said sharply. "He stays right here with me."

Kelsey wanted desperately to argue, but she released Bobby's hand. Just go along with him, she reminded herself. Give him the pills and let him leave. That's what Justin had told her to do.

Even so, giving in to his demands went against everything she believed in. She couldn't bear the thought of him taking Bobby out of her reach again. The only thing that made her comply was the knowledge that he could still take Bobby *and* the pills. This wasn't over yet. Not by a long shot.

She retrieved the duffel bag, then set it on the ground between them. Paul grabbed for it, took a quick look inside, then nodded with satisfaction.

"See, Kelsey, that wasn't so hard. We both end up with what we want." He glanced at Bobby and for just a second there was a hint of the old Paul in his expression, the faintest suggestion of real regret. "See you, son."

Bobby regarded his father with surprise. "You're going away again, Daddy?"

Paul nodded. "I've got to go back to Miami," he said, then briskly turned and headed for his car as if the past few days had been no more than a minor blip in his life.

Whatever had gone on the preceding few days, however frightened Bobby might have been at times, seemed to be forgotten. His face clouded over. "No, Daddy. Don't go."

Paul hesitated, then turned back. He knelt down and Bobby ran to him. Paul gathered him in a tight hug that brought the salty sting of tears to Kelsey's eyes. Whatever else she thought of her ex-husband, she knew his emotions now were genuine.

"'Bye, little buddy," Paul whispered, his voice breaking. "Remember that Daddy loves you, okay?"

Then he all but pushed Bobby in Kelsey's direction and sprinted to his car. Bobby began crying in earnest then and nothing Kelsey could do seemed to console him as they stood on the dusty, lonely road and watched Paul drive away.

"Oh, baby, it's going to be okay," she whispered, even as she heard sirens in the distance and knew that Justin's men were closing in on her ex-husband. She would do everything in her power to right Bobby's word, but she doubted Paul's would ever be the same again.

In that moment, she was able to recall with absolute clarity the man she had once loved so deeply, and all of the anger from the past few days died and gave way to regret.

"He's rolling, We're good to go." Justin's voice cut through the interminable silence as the radio crackled to life once more.

The deputy glanced toward Dylan. "You want in on this?"

Dylan thought of just how badly he wanted a piece of the arrest, but then he imagined Kelsey and

Bobby just up the road and what they must be feeling.

"No, but thanks," he said. He stepped from the car and held out his hand for his keys. The deputy returned them.

According to the last transmission Dylan had heard, Paul was still heading west, probably intending to loop around at some point and make his way back to the Dallas airport where he thought he could pick up his car. By now, that car was in some police impound lot, and if Justin had his way, Paul would get nowhere near the airport anyway.

Dylan hit the highway only a few car lengths behind the deputy who'd detained him. He pushed his speed to eighty, confident that there wasn't a cop in the vicinity who was interested in handing out a ticket at the moment.

He covered the few miles to the meeting point in less than ten minutes. He spotted Kelsey at the side of the road, Bobby in her arms. Both of them were crying. He pulled to a stop behind her car, then waited a minute to give them some privacy before getting out.

"Hey, darlin'," he called with forced cheer as he made his way to them.

Kelsey's gaze shot to his and he could see the relief in her eyes. Without relaxing her grip on her son, she reached out a hand to touch his face.

"You're okay?" she whispered. "Really?"

He winked at Bobby, who was staring at him wide-eyed, no doubt recalling the last time they'd met. "Not a scratch on me," he assured them both.

His gaze caught Kelsey's and held. "You did real good."

She almost faltered then, as if the last of her strength had finally deserted her. Dylan took Bobby from her, then circled her waist with his other arm.

"It's over, Kelsey. It's over and everything is going to be just fine."

"I want to believe that," she said as fresh tears spilled down her cheeks.

He gave her a squeeze. "Then believe it."

She sighed against him, then met his gaze. "I want to go home, Dylan. I just want to take my son and go home."

He nodded. "You still have that radio in the car?"

"On the seat."

"Let me okay it with Justin and we'll get out of here. Meantime, you hop on in the back with Bobby. I'll drive."

"What about your car?"

"I'll come back for it later." He picked up the transmitter and called Justin. "Mind if I take Kelsey on home? Can you catch up with us there?"

"Ten-four," Justin said.

"Everything okay on your end?" he asked, avoiding any direct mention of Paul or an arrest for Bobby's sake.

"Yep. We're on our way in now."

"Anybody get hurt?"

"Just their feelings," Justin said wryly. "He thought he was in the clear."

"Nice work. By the way, we'll talk about that clever little stunt you pulled with me later."

Justin laughed. ''I thought you might have something to say about that. Over and out, pal.''

Dylan glanced into the back seat and caught Kelsey's puzzled expression. An exhausted Bobby was sound asleep in her lap. Her hand rested protectively against his cheek as if she needed the contact to prove to herself he was with her again.

''What stunt?'' she asked quietly.

''Your buddy the sheriff had me pulled over about ten miles from here so I'd stay out of the way,'' he responded with a touch of indignation. ''I've got to admit it was a slick maneuver, though at the time I had a few choice words to say to him. Still, I wouldn't mind working for a man that devious.''

Kelsey laughed, her expression finally relaxing. ''Justin? Devious? Dylan, you've got to be kidding. He's a total straight-arrow.''

''That's what he wants you to think, but believe me, darlin', I know a sneaky scoundrel when I meet one.''

''It takes one to know one, I imagine.''

Dylan turned and pinned her with a look. ''You've got that right.'' He nodded toward Bobby. ''Think he'll be okay?''

''Time will tell. So far, it seems he genuinely believes he was just on a big adventure with his daddy and he's not completely happy about it being over. We'll have to wait and see if he starts having nightmares.''

''For what it's worth, I don't think Paul mistreated him,'' Dylan said. ''When I found him in that motel, he was more scared of me busting in there than he was of his dad. He even stood up to him, when Paul was tying me up. He told him I was Mommy's friend and he shouldn't do that.''

"That's my boy," she said with evident pride. "Quite a tough guy."

"Like his mama," Dylan noted, then asked sympathetically, "Reality setting in yet?"

"My knees haven't stopped knocking for the past ten minutes," she admitted.

"Then let's get home and get you something to eat and drink," he said as he started the car. "You'll need something to fortify you for all Justin's questions. This may be over, but there will be a ton of paperwork."

She chuckled lightly. "You're talking to a doctor, remember? The concept of paperwork is not alien to me. I can spend an hour pulling a kid through a medical crisis and another six hours filling out all the forms to justify the treatment. Does that make any sense?"

"It probably does if you're an insurance company, but to me, no. Paperwork is just one of the things that kept me out of the Houston police department."

"And the others?" she asked, studying him curiously.

"Rules," he said at once. "And more rules."

"I think I get the picture."

She fell silent and for a moment Dylan thought she, too, might have fallen asleep. A glance in the rearview mirror told him otherwise. She was staring at the passing scenery, though he doubted she was actually seeing it.

"Kelsey? What's up?"

"I was thinking," she said.

"About?"

"You, actually. We've just been through the most traumatic days of my life together. I feel closer to you than almost anyone else I can think of, and I don't really know you at all."

Dylan recognized the feeling. It had swept over him from time to time in the last few days. "How do you feel about changing that? Starting from scratch?"

"I don't think that's possible. We can't go back and pretend this didn't happen."

"No," he agreed. "But we can move on, fill in the blanks." He hesitated, then asked. "Or will I just be a reminder of everything that's gone on?"

"Absolutely not," she said fiercely. "How could I blame you for any of this?"

"I wasn't suggesting you'd blame me, just that you'd always link me to a bad time in your life, a time you'd rather not relive."

She shook her head. "No. Something good has to come out of all this. Maybe it's you and me."

Dylan felt something in his chest tighten at her words. He wanted to believe that just as badly as she did.

"Is that okay with you?" she asked, sounding suddenly hesitant. "I mean this hasn't exactly been a picnic for you, either. I know it's stirred up all sorts of old memories."

"No, it hasn't been a picnic, but it's opened my eyes to a lot of stuff. It's put me in touch with some feelings I'd tried to pretend didn't exist."

"Feelings about your son?"

"Yes."

"What will you do about them?"

Dylan reached a decision he'd been toying with for the past few days. "As soon as everything is wrapped up here, I'm going to see Kit."

"And?"

"I'm going to ask her to modify the custody arrangement."

Kelsey reached over the seat and squeezed his shoulder. "Oh, Dylan, I hope it works out for you."

"It will," he said fiercely. His gaze caught hers in the rearview mirror. "Because then I have to get back here and attend to some unfinished business."

Chapter Thirteen

The day had dragged on endlessly and Kelsey was clearly exhausted. Dylan could see it in her eyes and in the pallor of her complexion. She never took her gaze off Bobby, as if she feared letting him out of her sight, even though Paul was now in custody.

By the time the authorities had sorted out everything at the jail, then come by to take Kelsey's statement, it was pushing dinnertime. Her house was still crowded with visitors, most of whom had come bearing food they clearly had every intention of sticking around to share.

To Dylan's frustration, there was nothing he could do about any of it. It would take time to ease her fears. And at the rate the evening was progressing, it was going to take almost as long to get everyone out from underfoot. His occasional attempts to shoo a few well-wishers toward the door had been met with resistence, so he'd finally given up and retreated to the kitchen to grab a beer.

"What are you growling under your breath about?" Trish asked him, cornering him before he could even get the refrigerator door open.

He frowned at her. "Don't these people know when to go home?"

"They just want Kelsey to know they care."

"They can tell her that tomorrow. She's beat."

His sister studied him knowingly. "You're awfully protective of her. Do I detect more than a casual interest in her well-being?"

"The man's a goner," Jeb chimed in, joining them. "I doubt he's known which way was up since he met her."

Dylan glowered at his brother. "Watch it. I can have you on an oil rig in some very distant ocean with just one little hint to Dad."

"First you want to chain me to a desk, then you want to risk my neck on a rig. Make up your mind, big brother. I'm getting conflicting messages here."

"Bottom line, I'm looking for revenge," Dylan warned him. "Watch your step."

"It's not me you want revenge against," Jeb protested. He winked at their sister. "He'd like to wring Paul James's scrawny neck and he can't. It's got him frustrated." He cast an innocent look at Dylan. "Tell me again about how the man got the jump on you and tied you to a shower rod back in that motel."

"Okay, that's it," Dylan said. "It's the oil rig."

He deliberately glanced around the kitchen. "Where's my cell phone? I'm calling Dad."

Before he could place the call, Kelsey stepped into the kitchen and Dylan's pulse leapt into overdrive and all thoughts of revenge against either her ex-husband or his brother fled. He wanted very badly to haul her into his arms, but he didn't have the right. Not yet. And not in front of his nosy sister and meddlesome brother.

"What are you guys in here fussing and feuding about?" Kelsey asked. "I could hear you in the other room. Is this the Delacourt means of communicating?"

"Pretty much," Trish reported cheerfully. "Jeb's taunting Dylan, so Dylan's threatening to have Dad send him off to an oil rig. It's the usual stuff. Now that you're here to referee, I think I'll call it a night."

Dylan glanced pointedly at his brother. "You going with her?"

Jeb deliberately stayed right where he was. "I hadn't planned to."

"Change your plans," Dylan said grimly.

Jeb touched a lingering kiss to Kelsey's cheek that had Dylan seeing red.

"Guess I've got to run," Jeb told her. "Don't let big brother here bully you, the way he does us."

"Not a chance," Kelsey told him.

"If you need any tips on handling him, call me. I know all his dirty little secrets."

Kelsey chuckled, then gave Dylan a speculative once-over. "I had no idea you had any dirty little secrets."

"None worth mentioning," Dylan assured her, then scowled at his brother and sister. "Weren't you leaving?"

When Jeb and Trish were gone, Dylan shoved his hands in his pockets to keep from reaching for her. "I wouldn't even try to bully you, you know."

She laughed. "Sure you would. I'm not dumb enough not to know it's your nature to bully the people you care about." She studied him thoughtfully. "And you strike me as smart enough to know that it won't work with me."

"Duly noted." He nodded toward the living room. "Still mobbed in there?"

"It's thinning down some."

"Want me to clear the rest of them out?"

"No, I'm fine. I just can't seem to take my eyes off of Bobby for more than a second. I forced myself to come in here, just so I could break the pattern before it became a habit. Even at three, he'd hate me hovering."

Dylan stepped closer, crowding her. "And here I thought you came into the kitchen to see me."

She laughed again and Dylan realized how little reason she'd had for laughter in the last few days and what a pleasure it was to hear the sound of it.

"You're just a bonus," she told him.

Dylan met her gaze evenly, saw the laughter die on her lips, then the fire of desire in her eyes.

"Do you know how badly I want to kiss you right now?" he asked.

She swallowed hard before answering. "I have an inkling." Her chin rose a notch. "What are you going to do about it?"

The feisty tone made his pulse hum. "Why, doc, I think you're actually flirting with me. In fact, that almost sounded like a challenge. Is that possible?"

"Try me."

Dylan kept his hands jammed in his pockets as he lowered his head until his lips skimmed lightly over hers. Even so, he felt the shudder that washed through her. It was only a faint imitation of the one that rocked him when she leaned into the kiss, deepened it.

"Oh, baby," he murmured, "I have wanted this for so long."

"We've only known each other a few days," she reminded him before her breath hitched on a sigh.

"Forever," he corrected.

His arms went around her then and his mouth moved over hers, tasting, savoring, possessing. Heat spread through him with the speed and intensity of a flash fire.

With the one tiny little part of his brain that was still functioning he recognized this as a bad idea. It wasn't the time or the place to go into a passion-generated meltdown. In the aftermath of Bobby's rescue, Kelsey couldn't be thinking clearly, so it was up to him to do it.

In just a minute, he promised himself as he dipped his head for one more kiss. She had recently had a sip of wine and her lips were still cool, still bore its fruity taste. He doubted he would ever touch a glass of Chardonnay again without thinking of this moment.

He could feel himself growing hard, his erection as urgent and demanding as a randy teenager's, as hot and heavy as a man's. He knew he had to stop before he lost his last fragile thread of control.

Sighing, he pulled back, then stared into Kelsey's dazed eyes.

"Oh, my," she murmured, resting her forehead against his chest. "I've been married. I'm a doctor. I've read all the anatomy and human sexuality books. I understand how this works, but it has never, *never,* felt like this before."

Dylan grinned, nearly gave in to the temptation to swell right up with male pride. He had the sense not to delude himself that this was entirely personal, though. "Darlin', under the circumstances, what with all this adrenaline that's been pumping today, any man could have made your head reel."

"I don't think so."

"Trust me."

"I do," she said at once. "Just not about that."

"We'll try it again in a few days and see what you think."

Still frowning, she drew in a deep breath and gave him a curt nod. "I'll be looking forward to it," she said in a prim, businesslike tone that made him want to ravish her right then and there.

"I've got to get out of here," he muttered under his breath. This was dangerous turf, especially for two people who had a whole lot of thinking to do.

"Don't go," she pleaded. "Everyone will leave soon. Bobby will go to bed. I'm way too wired to sleep. I could use the company."

He scanned her face looking for evidence of just what she wanted the company for.

As if she'd read his mind, she smiled. "Just to talk, Dylan."

He nodded. "I can do that."

But it was going to be a whole lot harder than she could possibly guess.

Kelsey knew that Dylan was struggling with himself, that he wanted her every bit as much as she wanted him. She also recognized the danger in wanting something so badly under the circumstances. She certainly wasn't thinking clearly. Too much had happened in the last few days.

Still, she was reluctant to let him leave, even more reluctant to be alone with her thoughts. Her promise to do nothing more than talk had been made in haste, born of desperation. However, maybe by the time everyone else had gone home, after she'd tucked Bobby into his bed, she would have cooled down enough to stick to it.

"I'd better get in there and start saying goodbye. Maybe they'll take the hint," she said.

"You go. I'll hang out in here for a bit," Dylan said as he grabbed a beer from the refrigerator.

She walked back into the living room, scanning it for signs of Bobby. When she didn't spot him at once, her heart slammed against her ribs. She moved through the living room, then ran up the stairs to check his bedroom. He wasn't there, either. By the time she came back downstairs, her pulse was racing.

"Bobby! Where are you? Lizzy, Sharon Lynn, have either of you seen Bobby?"

Her shout brought Dylan from the kitchen.

"What is it?"

"I can't find Bobby," she said, nearing hysteria.

Lizzy rushed over, grabbed her in a tight hug. "Kelsey, it's okay. He's just outside with the other kids. They're playing hide-and-seek in the backyard."

"Are you sure?" she asked, her breathing not yet returning to normal.

"I'll check," Dylan said at once.

She was right on his heels. "I'll go with you."

He took her hand and she immediately felt calmer. But only when she spotted Bobby racing after Lizzy's son did her heartbeat slow. She sank down onto the top step and put her hands over her face. "Dear God, will I ever get past this?"

"Of course you will," Dylan said. "It's only been a few hours, darlin'. Nobody gets over having their kid taken that fast. Stop beating yourself up over a perfectly normal reaction."

She heard Bobby's laughter as he and some of the others tackled Jamey and began tickling him till he pleaded for mercy.

"How can it be so easy for him?" she wondered. "It's as if he hasn't even been away."

"All he knew was that he was away with his dad," Dylan reminded her. "He didn't know there was anything really wrong with that. Now he's just falling back into his usual routine. Be grateful, Kelsey. You wouldn't have wanted him to be traumatized by what happened."

"Of course not."

Bobby spotted her just then and ran across the

yard. He flung his arms around her. "Mommy, I love you."

Surprised by the impulsive and increasingly rare gesture, Kelsey squeezed him back, then forced herself to let go. Only after he was out of earshot did she whisper, "I love you, too, baby."

She allowed her shoulder to brush Dylan's as they sat on the back steps watching the kids play. He slid an arm around her waist, gave her a reassuring squeeze, then released her.

"They grow up so fast," she observed eventually. "One minute they're babies, the next they're all but grown…or think they are. Bobby's only three, but already I can feel the time flying by."

Only after her comment was greeted with total silence did she realize the impact it must have had on Dylan. She touched his cheek. "I'm sorry. I wasn't thinking."

"Don't worry about it. It's true. They do grow up way too fast. When I think of what I've missed with Shane, it makes me a little crazy. No more, though," he said with quiet resolve. "I'm not going to miss the rest of it."

She snuggled more tightly against his side, satisfied for the moment with no more contact between them than that. "Tell me what you remember most about him."

"What a tough little guy he was," he said at once. "There were some bigger kids in the neighborhood, but as soon as he could walk he wanted to play with them. He would fall down, get right back up and run even harder. He was the same way with his brothers."

Kelsey stared at him in surprise. "You mean his stepbrothers?"

"Technically, yes, but that's not how he thinks of them."

"You've seen them together? I thought you hadn't had any contact with him at all since you gave up custody?"

Dylan looked vaguely disconcerted that she had picked up on that. "I went by the house once, just to check on him," he said defensively. "I needed to see for myself that he was okay."

Somehow she found it reassuring that walking away hadn't been easy for him. "Of course you did. Were you satisfied?"

His expression glum, he nodded. "He looked happy. They looked like a real family."

"Was that the only time you saw him?"

"No," he admitted. "There was one time at his preschool. Kit spotted me that day. She sent me a finger painting he had done of his family. I guess she wanted to be sure I got the message."

"Or maybe she just wanted to reassure you that he was fine."

"Maybe."

"Dylan, can I ask you something?"

"Of course. After what we've been through the last few days, I think you've got a right to ask me just abut anything."

"What was your relationship with Kit like?"

He regarded her with surprise. "Are you sure you want to hear about that?"

"Why not? You know all the gory details of my relationship with Paul."

He nodded. "Fair enough. The truth is we never should have gotten married in the first place, even though we thought we were crazy in love with each other."

"Why not?"

"We were complete opposites in every conceivable way. That's probably why the attraction was so powerful, but in the end we couldn't find a middle ground on anything. We argued over everything. She liked pasta. I liked steak. She wanted to sleep in. I liked to get up at the crack of dawn. She preferred one toothpaste. I refused to give up the one I liked. At least with two tubes, we didn't have to fight over which way to squeeze the stuff out."

"Sounds like the usual marital kinks that get worked out with time," Kelsey said.

"Oh, that was the least of it. There were bigger issues, like my hours, the way I got caught up in a case and forgot about everything else. Before we had Shane, she was more tolerant of that. Afterward, she felt neglected and taken for granted and put upon. She was right. I didn't hold up my end of the marriage. But when she divorced me, I didn't like seeing all those faults listed on a court document, because I didn't want to believe I was to blame for our marriage failing. I wanted to blame her, so I accused her of being selfish and unwilling to compromise. I even tossed in a few accusations about other men. It got ugly."

"Was she seeing other men?"

He shrugged. "None I could prove, but I needed to believe that was the real reason she'd left me. I couldn't deal with the idea that she just didn't want me. When it didn't take her all that long to find someone new and marry again, I was convinced I'd been right all along.''

She met his gaze evenly. ''Is that really why you gave up custody of Shane? To punish yourself and her?''

''Of course not.''

''Are you sure?''

He sighed heavily. ''I don't know. Probably. I told myself it was the best thing for Shane and at the time, it probably was. Kit and I couldn't have a civil conversation.''

''Maybe now you can,'' Kelsey suggested.

''I hope so,'' he said fervently.

''When will you go to see her?''

''Tomorrow. Justin took Jeb out to get my car, so I'll be able to leave first thing in the morning.''

The thought of him leaving so soon was disconcerting. ''Tomorrow?'' she echoed, aware that she sounded dismayed.

He studied her intently. ''Okay, Kelsey, what's going on? Why do you sound so worried?''

''I guess I've just gotten used to you hanging around,'' she said mildly.

Looking very pleased, he looped his arm around her shoulders and planted a kiss on her cheek. ''Don't worry, darlin'. I'll be back. That's a promise.''

The intensity of his gaze disconcerted her almost as badly as the thought of him leaving. She glanced away, instinctively searching among the children until she spotted Bobby. He looked worn-out, which motivated her to leave Dylan's loose embrace.

"Okay, kids, that's it. It's time to call it a night."

"Aw, Mommy, not yet," Bobby protested.

"Yes. It's way past your bedtime. Everyone else has day camp tomorrow, too."

"I want to go to day camp."

"You're too little," Jamey Robbins pointed out.

"Am not little," Bobby retorted.

Dylan scooped him up before it could turn into a full-fledged battle. "Now you're bigger than he is," Dylan said as he settled Bobby on his shoulders.

"See," Bobby crowed. "I'm the biggest."

"You still can't go to day camp," Jamey told him and went indoors.

"Mommy," Bobby cried plaintively.

"What?"

"What's day camp?"

Kelsey bit back a grin. Typical kid. If someone he admired had something, he wanted it, too. It didn't matter that he didn't even know what it was.

"Day camp is a place kids go in the summer and learn stuff," Dylan told him. "Sort of like school. If you ask me, you're the lucky one. You get to stay home and play all day."

"Yeah," Bobby whooped. "I get to play!" He tugged on Dylan's hair. "Down. Gotta go tell Jamey."

As Bobby ran off, Kelsey chuckled. "Well, you've certainly given him the momentary edge. Thanks."

Then with Dylan's help she shooed the remaining pint-sized guests inside and matched them with their respective parents. Once the exodus started, it didn't take long to clear the place.

"Up to bed," she told Bobby.

He hesitated and she sensed suddenly that it wasn't just his usual reluctance to see the day end.

"What's up, pal? Want me to come up with you?"

He shook his head, then gazed shyly at Dylan. "Are you gonna be here in the morning?"

"Nope. I'm going away for a few days."

"Oh," Bobby said glumly.

Dylan hunkered down in front of him. "Why? Was there something you wanted to do tomorrow?"

"I was thinking maybe if you were here you could play with me. I got lots of neat stuff in the backyard."

Kelsey exchanged a puzzled look with Dylan.

"Why did you want Dylan to play with you, sweetie?"

"So Daddy can't make me go away again," he said simply.

Tears welled up in Kelsey's eyes. She had to turn away to keep Bobby from seeing. She was aware of Dylan quietly reassuring Bobby that his daddy wasn't going to take him again, but all the while her heart was breaking.

She felt Dylan's light touch on her arm and jerked her head toward him. "What?"

"I'm going to take Bobby up to bed and hang out for a minute, if it's okay with you."

Unable to speak around the lump in her throat, she simply nodded. Dylan squeezed her hand and mouthed, "He's going to be fine."

But Kelsey wasn't so sure. Would any of them ever really be fine again?

Chapter Fourteen

Dylan spent nearly a half hour talking to Bobby, trying to ease his fears, then tucking him into bed and waiting until he drifted off to sleep. All the while, he kept thinking of all the nights he'd missed doing exactly the same thing with Shane, all the stories he could have read to his son, all the sleepy talks they could have shared. The experience reinforced his decision to see Kit as soon as possible the next day. He wanted his son back in his life. He needed to be a dad again. Even part-time would be better than nothing.

As he went back downstairs, though, his thoughts shifted back to the woman waiting for him. He had seen her shattered expression when Bobby had revealed his fear of being taken away again by his dad. The fact that she had allowed him to step in and reassure the boy, then put him to bed, told Dylan just how distraught she had been. She'd been afraid Bobby would detect her own fear.

Obviously, she had been wanting to believe, just as he had, that Bobby hadn't been affected by the events of the last few days. Now they could no longer delude themselves. He'd been able to step in tonight, but what if Bobby needed more help than either he or Kelsey could give him?

Dylan walked into the living room to find Kelsey curled up at one end of the sofa. She hadn't turned on the lights and the room was in shadows.

"Is he okay?" she asked, sounding lost and defeated.

"Sound asleep," Dylan reassured her as he crossed the room, sat down beside her and drew her into his arms. She came willingly.

"Oh, Dylan, I wanted so badly for him to have come through this unscathed."

"To tell you the truth, I think he was just worried about leaving you again. I don't think it had anything to do with him being frightened of his father."

"But he saw Paul shoot that gun in the air and tie you up. How could he not have been terrified? I must have been crazy to think he would forget all about it just like that."

"We talked about that. I told him nothing really bad happened, that it was like a game between his dad and me to see who would get to bring him back to you fastest. He seemed to accept that."

"In other words, you lied to him. Is that good?"

"It's better than telling him his dad did a terrible thing that could have had tragic consequences. He'll figure that out for himself when he's older. For now, I think it's better just to ease his mind. Maybe you should talk to a psychologist. See what he says.''

''Of course,'' she said, sounding relieved to have something concrete she could do. ''I don't know why I didn't think of that. It's exactly what I'd recommend to the parent of any patient of mine who'd been through a traumatic experience. I'll call a friend of mine in Miami first thing in the morning. I just wish I had some answers now.''

''Bobby's sound asleep. The answers can wait until morning.'' He gave her a knowing look. ''But just in case you don't see it that way, my guess is you have a few psych books left over from med school tucked away somewhere around here.''

She brightened at the suggestion. ''In the attic.'' She started to get up.

''Not just yet,'' Dylan said, holding her a little more tightly. ''Let's talk about you for a minute. Will you be able to sleep tonight or are you going to spend the whole night running into Bobby's room just to make sure he's there?''

''I'll try to limit it to once an hour,'' she said candidly.

He debated asking his next question, then decided to make the offer anyway. ''Would it help if I stayed here? On the sofa,'' he elaborated before she could jump to the wrong conclusion.

Her hesitation suggested she badly wanted to resist the idea, that she was used to handling crises on her own and needed to start doing that again. Finally she released a soft sigh. ''Would you mind?''

''I offered, didn't I?''

Her gaze clashed with his. "Not on the sofa, though. Upstairs. With me."

Dylan's heart beat a little faster, but he shook his head. "Bad idea."

"Why?"

"We won't sleep, Kelsey, and you know it."

"Would that be so terrible?"

Dylan struggled with himself, with his sense of honor. "I thought we'd decided not to rush into anything."

"It's just sex, Dylan, not a commitment."

She uttered the words so damned bravely, but they both knew better. She didn't have casual relationships, and though he'd had his share, he knew this wasn't going to be one of them. She deserved better from him.

"You're wrong," he told her. "You don't have casual flings and when it comes to someone like you, neither do I. I want to make something of what we have, Kelsey. I don't want to mess it up by getting into something heavy at the wrong time, when you're vulnerable. I don't want you waking up in the morning with regrets."

"I'm stronger than I seem, Dylan. You've seen me at my worst. Believe me, under normal circumstances, I'm perfectly capable of making a rational decision."

He laughed. "Oh, I'm certain of that, darlin', but you're not thinking with your brain just now."

She stared at him indignantly, then chuckled self-consciously. "Shouldn't that be my line?"

"I'll give you a rain check to use it on me," he promised. "Now scoot before I change my mind and decide I can't resist ravishing you, after all. You can hunt for that psychology book and read yourself to sleep with all that dull, dry material.''

She regarded him with obvious regret. ''You're not going to be noble forever, are you?''

Dylan laughed, despite the ache that was already building with no immediate relief in sight. ''No, darlin'. I think you can count on me getting past this in no time at all.''

To Kelsey's amazement, after checking on Bobby only twice and reading just a few pages of the child-psychology textbook she'd found in the attic, she actually fell soundly asleep and slept through the rest of the night. She knew she owed that to Dylan's presence downstairs. While the rational part of her brain knew that Paul couldn't come after their son again, on another level she had feared he would somehow find a way out of jail and do just that. Having Dylan there to stop him had relieved her illogical worries.

The man was definitely one of the good guys. She had recognized his strength from the beginning, but she was just now beginning to understand how deep his integrity ran. Last night she had found his sense of honor inconvenient, but today she was grateful for it. She had been caught up in an adrenaline rush, no doubt about it.

One thing she knew, though, the attraction she had developed toward Dylan Delacourt wasn't going away. If anything, it was growing deeper day by day. Sometimes, with some people, a lifetime of getting acquainted could be crammed into a few short days. It had been with them.

Down the hall she could hear Bobby thumping around in his room, probably tossing half his toys on the floor in search of the one buried deepest in the pile. The sound brought a smile to her lips.

Then she heard Dylan stirring downstairs and her smile spread.

She took a quick shower, tugged on a clean outfit, then poked her head into Bobby's room. He was sitting on his bed, totally absorbed in his favorite picture book, one with lots of fire engines and police cars in it. He gave her a distracted wave and went right back to it.

Back to normal, she told herself with a relieved sigh. At least that was the way it seemed right now. Hard to tell what the day would bring.

Downstairs, she could smell the coffee brewing as she walked toward the kitchen. She found Dylan with one jeans-clad hip propped against the counter, his shirt hanging open and a cup of coffee in his hand. He looked sleepy and rumpled and indescribably sexy. His expression brightened when he saw her.

"Good morning."

Staring at his partially bared chest, she murmured something that was probably incomprehensible. Finally she tugged her gaze away and looked into eyes dancing with amusement.

"Never seen a male body up close before?" he teased.

"Most of the ones I see are under twelve. Trust me, it's not the same."

"Speaking of that, you aren't planning to go back to work today, are you?"

"I was thinking about going in later. Why?"

"What about Bobby?"

"Hank's invited him out to the ranch after day camp today to play with Jamey. I figured he'd rather do that than stay here with me."

"Are you okay with that?"

"I'll have to be sometime."

"*Sometime* is not necessarily today," he pointed out.

"Dylan, I have to do this my own way."

He appeared to bristle a bit at that. "Well, of course you do, but I was just worried...."

"No need for you to worry," she insisted. "Not anymore."

He leveled a look straight at her. "That's like asking me not to breathe. I'm the oldest of five. Worrying is what I do best." He grinned ruefully. "It always drove Trish, Jeb and the others crazy, too. I can't get over it, though, so you might as well get used to it."

"Then add me to the list of those who find it annoying, but endearing," Kelsey told him, then stood on tiptoe to press a kiss to his cheek to take the sting out of her words. "Thanks for caring."

Having someone concerned about her well-being, challenging her independence at every turn, was going to take a whole lot of getting used to. But seeing the flare of heat in Dylan's eyes, feeling the responding warmth steal through her, she knew it was also going to be worth it.

* * *

That peck on the cheek was the best Dylan got from Kelsey before he took off, but in some ways it was better than the most passionate kisses they had shared. There was a lighthearted teasing about it, an underlying affection that he couldn't mistake. It was exactly what he intended to build on...as soon as he had his own life settled.

First he drove by the sheriff's office to check in with Justin and assure himself that Paul wasn't going anywhere anytime soon.

"Listen, there's something I've been wanting to talk to you about," Justin said, gesturing toward the chair opposite his desk.

Dylan studied him worriedly as he sat. "You're not still agitating about me coming after Paul yesterday and almost busting into that meeting you had staked out, are you?"

"No more than you're still ticked that I stopped you," Justin retorted.

"Okay, let's call it a draw. What's on your mind?"

"I could use another man around here, someone with real experience and good instincts. Interested?"

"I'm a private investigator. What makes you think I'd want to become a sheriff's deputy?"

"Call me crazy, but I got the distinct impression you were interested in a certain baby doc who's new in town. Am I wrong?"

Dylan hesitated, then shook his head. "You're not wrong."

"What do you intend to do about it?"

"I'm not real sure that's any of your business."

Justin scowled. "Kelsey's like family. That

makes it my business. You can either answer to me or answer to Grandpa Harlan. Believe me, I'm the better bet. He tends to get real pushy.''

Dylan actually appreciated the strength of that particular bond. He knew from his own experience with his brothers and his sister that that kind of protectiveness ran deep. Hadn't he explained that very concept to Kelsey the night before?

''I have some things to work out,'' he finally admitted. ''Then I intend to come back here and see how things go from there.''

''Wouldn't that be a whole lot easier if you had a steady paycheck?''

''My business does real well,'' Dylan said.

''In Houston. How well will it do if you're here?''

To Dylan's regret, Justin had a point. ''I guess I hadn't gotten quite that far along with my thinking,'' he conceded. ''Give me a little time. I'll consider the offer.''

''Take as much time as you need.''

Dylan stood up and offered Justin his hand. ''Thank you for letting me work with you on this case. I would much rather work with the authorities than butt heads with them.''

''Which is exactly why I think you'd fit in here.''

Dylan thought about the proposal all the way over to Trish's. While it had some merit, he still wasn't sure he was suited to following a bunch of rules and regulations, even with a decent guy like Justin as his boss.

When he got to his sister's, he found her in the kitchen and discovered that Jeb was packing to go back to Houston.

"Where's my best girl?" Dylan demanded as he poured himself a cup of coffee.

"Upstairs with Jeb. Be careful. I think she's defecting. You haven't been around much the past couple of days and I suspect her heart's fickle."

"Not my sweet Laura," he said loudly enough to be heard upstairs.

"Unca Dyl." The delighted cry echoed through the house and was quickly followed by the thunder of tiny feet heading for the stairs.

"Whoa, there, sweetheart," Jeb shouted, pounding after her.

A moment later, he came into the kitchen with Laura sitting on his shoulders. Their niece's arms were already outstretched for Dylan.

Trish chuckled. "Told you she was fickle."

Jeb handed Laura over, then surveyed Dylan. "You look like hell. No sleep?"

"I got plenty of sleep," Dylan told him. "Unfortunately the sofa was too blasted short. I've got aches and pains everywhere."

"And here I envisioned you over there—"

"Careful, pal."

Jeb grinned. "Celebrating, big brother. That's all I was going to say. Where did you think I was going?"

"Never can tell with you."

"Can I hitch a ride back to Houston with you or should I call Dad and ask to have the corporate jet sent over?" Jeb asked, wisely changing the subject.

"I'll take you," Dylan said.

Trish stared at him in shock. "You're going back to Houston today?"

He nodded.

"But I thought…"

"Well, you thought wrong. I have things to do."

Her gaze narrowed. "Such as?"

"I'll let you know next time I see you."

"When will that be?"

He frowned at her. "Why all the questions?"

"It's just that I saw how you and Kelsey were together. I was sure something was going to happen."

Dylan sighed. "Saints protect me from the busybodies in this town. You're the second person today who wanted to poke around in my private life."

"Because I care," Trish said huffily. "You certainly don't hesitate to poke and prod when the mood suits you. Never mind, though. I don't have to follow your example. I'll keep my mouth shut from now on."

Dylan exchanged a look with Jeb and they both burst out laughing.

"That will be the day, baby sister," Dylan said, then kissed her. "We forgive you, though. Just rein it in for a few days, okay?"

She seized on that. "A few days? That's it?"

He nodded.

"I can last a few days," she said briskly, then grinned at him. "Can Kelsey?"

Dylan frowned at her. "Watch it, kid."

"Just checking," she said innocently.

Damn, Dylan thought. How was he going to figure out the rest of his life with half the world watching his every move? He realized Justin and Trish were only the tip of the iceberg. He still had to drive all the way to Houston with Jeb in that car, then be subjected to the curiosity of his other brothers, his father and, worst of all, his mother.

There were occasions—and this was clearly destined to be one of them—when he deeply regretted being part of a large family that insisted on knowing everything about his life practically before he did.

Then again, turnabout was only fair play. He'd been doing the same thing to all of them for years.

Chapter Fifteen

Kelsey couldn't concentrate. She'd done nearly a dozen preschool physicals since noon, returned nearly as many calls, and organized her schedule so she could catch up on all the appointments she'd missed while Bobby had been missing. Even at that, she kept thinking about Dylan and the promise that had been in his eyes and in his voice when he'd left her.

Could something so important be this easy? Could she possibly fall in love in the blink of an eye in the midst of the worst crisis of her life? Or was she just confusing love with relief and gratitude? Dylan was obviously worried that she might be doing just that and she supposed he was right to be so concerned. It wasn't something to make a mistake about. They both had past mistakes to serve as warnings against making hasty judgments.

She leaned back in her chair and thought about the kisses they'd shared. She was still daydreaming, a smile on her lips, when Lizzy poked her head in.

"You ready to grab some lunch?" she asked, then did a double take. "Or would you rather tell me what put that smile on your face?" She came in and sat down, clearly making her own choice about which took precedence. "Dylan, I suppose."

"Why ask when you think you already know the answer?"

"Because, contrary to all the rumors, I'm not infallible. Sometimes my diagnoses are off."

"Not a smart thing for a doctor to admit to," Kelsey teased. "Malpractice suits being what they are these days."

"Don't remind me." Her expression sobered. "How's Bobby doing? I didn't get to see him before I left the ranch today."

"Overall, he's doing a whole lot better than I would have predicted. Even so, first thing this morning I called that child psychologist we liked so much back in med school. You remember the one?"

"Handsome Harry?" Lizzy recalled.

"We liked him because he was brilliant."

"Yeah, right," Lizzy teased. "Who actually noticed that?"

"I did," Kelsey insisted. "And so did you, so stop it. He agreed with Dylan that Bobby's probably more worried about me leaving again than about his dad coming back. Bobby had one bad spell last night right before bed, but Dylan talked to him and that seemed to do the trick. He slept straight through the night.''

"Dylan, huh? He's still spending a lot of time around the house, even though his job is done?''

"Don't look at me like that,'' Kelsey protested. "It's not like he spent the night. Well, he did, but—''

"Oh, really?''

"Lizzy, cut it out.''

"He's a great guy.''

"Yes, he is,'' Kelsey agreed. "And he was a rock during all of this, but he has his own issues to deal with and so do I. The timing's all off.''

"Today, maybe,'' Lizzy noted. "How about tomorrow?''

"We'll see.'' It was as much of a commitment as Kelsey was prepared to make until she and Dylan could have some time together to sort things out.

Dylan sat outside Kit's house and mentally rehearsed what he intended to say to persuade her to have the custody agreement amended. He needed to have every argument in place, needed to remain absolutely calm. Anything else and he would blow his best chance at getting back into Shane's life. He could always go to court, but this way was preferable. Funny how a little maturity could make things a whole lot clearer.

He'd arrived without any advance warning, figuring that the element of surprise was on his side. Kit's defenses would be down and she would be alone without her new husband there to shore up any protests she might have initially.

"It's now or never, pal," he muttered under his breath. He got out of the car and walked across the street. Kit had the front door open before he could knock.

"I was wondering when you were going to decide to come in," she said, meeting his gaze evenly. She didn't seem especially surprised to see him. Nor did she seem as dismayed or angry as he'd anticipated.

"I see your radar's as good as ever," he said, managing a grin to take any sting out of the words. "You look good, Kit. Great, in fact."

"Are you trying to butter me up for something, or do you mean it?" she asked, studying him thoughtfully. "You actually mean it, don't you?"

He nodded. "Is that such a big surprise?"

"You rarely noticed how I looked while we were married, not after the first year, anyway."

The truth hurt. "I'm sorry," he said, meaning it.

She shrugged. "It's in the past. I'm happy now. How about you?"

"I'm getting there. There's just one thing missing."

She regarded him evenly, then sighed. "I've been expecting this. Come into the kitchen. Can I get you some iced tea or some lemonade? You used to like that."

Relieved that she hadn't gone ballistic right off the bat, he nodded. "Lemonade would be great."

She poured the drink into a tall glass filled with ice just the way he liked it, then handed it to him. Rather than sitting, though, she stood by the counter, watching him warily.

"Okay, out with it," she said.

He was surprised by her demand. "Were you always this direct? I don't remember that."

"No," she said. "I learned from my mistakes. Maybe if I'd told you what I needed a whole lot sooner, we wouldn't be where we are today."

The comment stunned him. It was the first time he could recall her being willing to share any of the blame for what went wrong in their marriage.

"I don't know," he said honestly. "I probably still wouldn't have known the meaning of compromise."

She laughed. "You really were used to being king of the roost in that family of yours, weren't you? Big brother could do no wrong."

"Is that how you saw it?"

"That's how it was," she said without rancor. "And they might fight you tooth and nail over anything and everything, but heaven forbid anyone else should question your decisions. It was daunting."

He tried hard to remember that part of the past, but all he recalled was the mounting tension between him and Kit and his inability to do anything to lessen it.

"I'm sorry for that, too," he told her.

She shook her head. "Amazing. Two apologies in one day, when I didn't think you were capable of any."

"I'm—"

She held up her hand. "Enough. Why are you here, Dylan? It's not to take a walk down memory lane."

He took a deep breath and dived in. "I've been

thinking a lot about Shane lately.'' He looked into her eyes. ''Wondering if I made a mistake.''

''He's happy, Dylan.''

''I know that,'' he said, fighting against an unreasonable tide of misery. Was he wrong to be asking this of Kit? Of Shane? Was it too late to stake a claim he never should have given up in the first place?

''But you miss him, anyway,'' she guessed.

''Yes. Does that make me totally selfish?''

''No. Sorry. It just makes you human. You're his dad, Dylan. He's the best thing you ever gave me. I'm not surprised you want to know him. I would, if our roles were reversed.''

He began to feel hopeful. ''Can we work this out? Or is it too late?''

She regarded him with surprising sympathy. ''As long as we're still alive, it's never too late to change things. Another lesson learned through our mistakes.''

''I don't want to turn his life upside down, or yours and Steve's.''

''Oh, Dylan, knowing his real dad loves him isn't going to turn his world upside down. It's just going to bring more love into his life. Steve and his boys taught me that when they accepted Shane and me right from the beginning. You're the one who was so certain Shane would be better off without you. I never thought it. Not really. Neither did Steve, though he was grateful to you for wanting him to be a real dad to Shane. I always hoped you'd realize one day what you'd given up.''

He stared at her in amazement. He could tell that

she honestly meant what she'd said, that whatever ill will had been between them was in the past. "You're a remarkable woman, Kit. Why didn't I know that?"

"Maybe I did my best to see that you never saw it," she said wryly. She glanced at the clock. "Shane will be home soon. Want to stick around?"

"More than anything," Dylan admitted, then felt panic clawing at his insides. What if he'd waited too long? What if Shane didn't even know who he was? Would he be able to bear it? "Maybe we should do this another day. Shouldn't you talk to Steve first? Maybe a lawyer?"

"This is between you and me and Shane," she said. "The legalities can be worked out later. As for Steve, we agreed from the beginning that if you ever changed your mind, we'd amend the agreement. Frankly, what surprised us both—especially after those surreptitious little visits of yours—was that it took you so long."

He shook his head at her ability to read him so well. "Why didn't you just knock me upside the head back then and tell me what a mistake I was making?"

"Would you have listened?"

"Probably not," he admitted.

"Which is exactly why it seemed like such a waste of time. Besides, I'll admit to being selfish enough back then to want Shane all to myself. I figured you didn't deserve him."

Just then Dylan heard the rumble of what was most likely a school bus outside. His pulse accelerated.

"Is that him?"

Kit nodded. "Prepare to be caught up in a tornado."

Less than a minute later, the front door opened, then slammed shut.

"Mommy!" The excited shout just about raised the rafters. "I'm home!"

"In the kitchen, Shane."

"Baking cookies?" he asked hopefully as he ran into the room, then skidded to a stop at the sight of Dylan. He inched closer to his mother, eyeing Dylan warily. Kit kept a light hand resting on his shoulder, but said nothing. Dylan was at a loss for words.

"I know you," Shane said after what seemed like an eternity. He looked up at Kit. "Don't I?"

She nodded.

"You're the man in the picture."

Dylan felt as if his heart had stopped. "What picture is that?"

"In my room. Mommy told me it was my dad, my real dad. She said Steve adopted me, so he's a real dad, too. She said I'm really lucky to have two dads."

Dylan felt the sharp sting of tears in his eyes and blinked them away. If he and Kit had been alone at that moment, he might have bawled like a baby, he was so grateful to her for keeping him alive in Shane's mind. He glanced up at her and mouthed silently, "Thank you."

Shane tilted his head in a way that was pure Delacourt and studied Dylan. "Am I right? Are you my dad?"

Dylan nodded. "I am." He hesitated, then asked,

"Would you mind if I gave you a hug? I've really, really missed you."

"I guess."

Shane said it with the obvious reluctance and distaste of a typical boy his age. It was such a normal reaction, Dylan almost laughed. He knelt down, opened his arms and waited until Shane came to him. If it had been up to him, the hug would have lasted forever, but he knew Shane couldn't possibly understand why such a simple gesture meant so much to him that he wanted it to go on and on.

The instant Dylan released him, Shane turned to his mother. "So, did you bake cookies today or not?"

"Chocolate chip," Kit said, sounding as emotional as Dylan felt. "They're in the cookie jar. Take two."

Shane darted to the counter, climbed up on a step stool and reached for the cookie jar. He came out with a handful of cookies. Grinning, he held them toward Dylan. "You want some? Mom makes the best chocolate chip cookies in the world."

"I remember." He accepted the cookies, then asked, "Are these your favorites?"

"Pretty much. How about you?"

"Definitely." There were a thousand other things he wanted to know, a thousand questions to be asked, but he knew he'd have to ease into this new relationship, give all of them time to adjust.

With Kit staying in the background, they munched their cookies in companionable silence. Dylan felt the situation called for something momentous, but maybe sharing chocolate chip cookies with his son was exactly right. He figured a fireworks display and whoops of joy would have put the boy off. This was—he searched for the right word—this was a beginning, he concluded. He knew, too, that he couldn't have asked for—much less deserved—anything more.

"Mommy, can I go outside now?" Shane asked, already anticipating a positive response and heading toward the back door.

Kit nodded. "In the yard or, if you want to ride your bike, on the sidewalk out front. Nowhere else, okay?"

"Got it," Shane said. At the door, he glanced back at Dylan. "Are you gonna be my dad for real from now on?"

"I'd like that very much."

"Do I have to go away with you?"

"No," Dylan said, thinking of another little boy who'd been taken from his home all too recently. "I'll come here, if it's okay with you and your mom and dad."

"Will you bring me stuff sometimes?"

"Shane!" Kit protested.

"Well, Jimmy's real dad brings him presents all the time."

Dylan winked at him. "Oh, I think you can count on me bringing you things from time to time, if your mom says it's okay."

A smile spread across Shane's face. "Two dads. This is so cool."

And then he bounded out the door, letting it slam behind him.

Just like that, as if in answer to a prayer, Dylan

had his son back. And it was all because of Kelsey and another little boy who'd come into his life and made him see what he'd given up.

He knew then that he didn't want to wait, couldn't wait to bring the two of them into his life forever. Waiting could cost a man everything that really mattered. He would never risk that kind of loss again.

Dylan impulsively stopped and bought the biggest diamond in the jewelry store on the way back to Los Piños. Kelsey was probably figuring he'd start out slow, maybe ask for a date. He intended to go for the gold right from the start.

He found her at the clinic, surrounded by kids getting preschool physicals. He shuddered at the number already clutching lollipops as proof that they'd bravely withstood their shots. Kelsey caught sight of him in the waiting room and stumbled over whatever she'd been about to say to the mother standing with her. Then she deliberately glanced down at the chart in her hand, gathered her composure and went on as if he weren't there. As soon as mother and child were on their way, she beckoned to him.

"Mr. Delacourt, come on into my office." She smiled at the remaining patients. "This won't take long."

Dylan followed her into her office, then shut the door. He studied her in her crisp white lab coat and decided she looked just as sexy in that as she did in those shorts she'd worn around the house. Apparently he was going to get turned on no matter what she wore. Good thing, too, given what he was planning for their future.

"You're back sooner than I expected," she said, moving behind her desk as if to keep a safe distance between them.

"I couldn't stay away."

"How did things go with Kit?"

"I'll tell you about it later. Have dinner with me."

"I can't," she said too quickly. "I shouldn't leave Bobby again tonight."

Dylan regarded her intently. "You're not getting nervous about being alone with me, are you?"

"Of course not," she retorted indignantly, but there were bright patches of color on her cheeks.

"Tsk, tsk, doc. Fibbing doesn't suit you."

"You come to dinner at my house tonight," she countered as if that would prove her bravery.

"With Bobby as chaperone? How convenient," he taunted.

Her chin rose at that. "He has a very early bedtime."

Dylan grinned. "Things are looking up. How about you, darlin'? Do you have an early bedtime?"

She stared at him. "What has gotten into you?"

"I'm a man on a mission."

The statement clearly disconcerted her. "What sort of a mission?"

"You'll find out soon enough."

"Tell me now. I'm an impatient woman."

"Here? You want me to tell you here, in your office, with all those people just outside?" He followed her behind her desk, leaned down until his mouth hovered over hers.

"Mmm-hmm," she murmured.

"I was thinking more along the lines of something with moonlight and roses, but if you say so…"

She swallowed hard. "Dylan, what…this isn't about…you're not going to…"

He touched a finger to her lips. "Hush. Let me say it."

"I don't think—"

"It's not the time or the place," he agreed. "But what the heck? We're an unconventional pair. We do things our own way. Why not ask you to marry me in your office, especially now that I've seen just how cute you are in that lab coat?"

"Marry you?" she echoed, clearly stunned. "You're asking me to marry you? Are you serious?"

He waved the jewelry box under her nose, then gestured for her to take it. "See for yourself."

She put her hands behind her back as if she didn't dare. Dylan opened the box instead. Kelsey gasped. Her eyes widened in wonder.

"You are serious."

"Every bit as serious as one of those needles you've been poking around with today."

"Why? What?" Her gaze searched his face. "Dylan, are you sure?"

"That I love you? Yes. Absolutely. Seeing Shane again also made me see that I don't want to waste any more of my life being separated from the people I love. You're one of those people. You and Bobby."

"Just like that?" she asked incredulously.

He nodded. "Just like that."

She shook her head as if to clear it. "Dylan, I can't think."

"Don't think. Feel. What do you feel right now?"

"Overwhelmed," she said at once. "Dizzy."

He tucked a finger under her chin, waited for her to meet his gaze. "And?"

"In love," she whispered. "I don't understand why or how it happened so fast, but it's true. I love you."

"Then can you think of a single reason to wait?"

"I can think of a million reasons to wait," she said, regarding him with mock severity. Then a smile spread across her face. "But not a one of them really matters."

"Then we're on? You'll marry me?"

"Yes," she sighed against his lips. "Oh, yes."

"If there weren't a whole waiting room full of people out there, I would make love to you right here and now," he told her.

"I could get rid of them," she offered.

"But you won't. You're entirely too responsible. I admire that, usually. I can wait until later."

"Tonight?"

"Or our wedding night," he suggested. "Maybe that should be the one traditional thing we do."

"Tonight," she repeated very firmly.

Dylan laughed at the prospect of two control freaks butting heads from now through eternity. "If you say so, darlin'," he said, proving that he'd very recently learned the art of compromise.

"I say so," she said, seizing the last word.

He figured he'd let her get away with it...this time.

Epilogue

Impulsiveness could only go so far. Kelsey made Dylan wait for two months before walking down the aisle. She insisted there were too many things to be settled, such as whether he was going to accept Justin's offer to work as a deputy sheriff and which brand of toothpaste they were going to use. She wanted all of those pesky little details ironed out before the ceremony. She intended to start their married life in blissful unanimity.

Of course, things got a little crazy when it came time to decide on how big a wedding to have. Harlan Adams won out with his bid for a lavish affair, held in the same church where all of the Adamses had been wed. There were two ring bearers—Bobby and Shane—two maids of honor—Lizzy and Trish—and a whole slew of ushers. Jeb was the best man.

As for the honeymoon, with Bobby staying safely at Lizzy's Dylan had refused to tell her a single thing. He'd swept her away from the ceremony, escorted her to the Delacourt Oil corporate jet, and for most of the trip he'd plied her with champagne and kisses to keep her questions to a minimum. After a while she hadn't much cared if they wound up on a beach in Hawaii or in a snowbank in Alaska. Or stayed at thirty thousand feet.

"We are not making love for the first time in a jet," Dylan declared eventually, drawing away with obvious reluctance.

"Why not? The idea of flying high on love doesn't suit such a staid individual as yourself?"

"Staid? Me?" He regarded her indignantly.

She reached for the top button on his shirt and slowly undid it. "Prove me wrong," she challenged. She leaned forward and ran the tip of her tongue over his lower lip. He shuddered.

"Kelsey."

His protest sounded a lot like a moan, so she decided to put a little more effort into getting him to loosen up. She worked the next button loose and caressed his upper lip with her tongue, then dipped inside his mouth until they were both gasping for breath.

There was a lot to be said for surprising Dylan with her inventiveness. It was having a very provocative effect on her own libido, too. She'd never had the time or the lighthearted daring to experiment with her own sexuality with Paul. Dylan seemed to welcome it, even if he was somewhat bemused by it. In fact, he was beginning to look downright dazed.

"Doesn't this fancy jet have a bed?" she inquired, gazing around at the luxurious interior and concluding that this was a life-style she could get used to.

"I doubt there's been much need for one before now," Dylan said dryly. "It's mostly used for business trips."

"Don't the Delacourt men ever rest?"

"Not so you'd notice."

"Too bad," she said, then tried a release button to see just how far the seat would go back. "Not bad," she observed when Dylan was all but prone. His eyes widened as she inched over to join him.

"Kelsey, I really don't think…"

"Ssh." She touched a finger to his lips. "This isn't about thinking. It's about discovery and exploration. Since you're part of an oil family, those terms should be familiar."

"I'm a private investigator," he reminded her, though a smile was building at the corners of his mouth.

"Then investigate," she said boldly, sitting up so she was straddling him.

"Oh, baby," he murmured, but his hands fumbled with the buttons on her blouse, then made short work of her bra.

His heated gaze settled on her breasts with such longing that she could feel the nipples tighten into hard little buds. When his mouth closed over one, she sucked in a shocked breath, then moaned with pure pleasure. "Oh, Dylan," she said with a sigh. "I want you so much."

"Since I could never deny you anything, I guess that means we make love here and now," he said with feigned resignation. "Are you really sure you don't want to wait for fancy sheets and buckets of champagne?"

She picked up her glass and dribbled a few drops of champagne on his chest, then leaned down and slowly licked them up. "There's more than enough champagne right here to make things interesting."

"Kelsey, I've gotta admit this is a side of you I never imagined."

She laughed at his perplexed expression. "Hey, I grew up playing doctor, remember? How about you?"

"Not once," he admitted.

"Then now's your chance. I'll let you know if you're getting it right."

"I'm so glad I have an expert on hand to advise me."

"Something tells me you'll be a very apt pupil," she said as his hands moved from her breasts to her hips, then began working on the snap of her slacks. Desire took away the last of her breath as she gave in to sensation—heating skin, slick caresses, intimate kisses.

She murmured praise and yearning in a mix that quickly turned to almost incoherent pleas as the coil of tension inside her spiraled tighter and tighter. Only when she was at the very edge did

Dylan lift her hips, then settle her over him until he was deep inside.

Complete, she thought with amazement. This was what it felt like to be whole, to know the wonder of being one with another person. How had she not known about this in all the years she and Paul had rushed through sex, fitting it into a schedule already filled to bursting with other commitments? That was why, of course. They had had no leisure, no time or inclination for the pure enjoyment of each other's bodies. How terribly sad, she thought right before she gave herself completely to wicked sensation.

Yet how right that she was discovering this now with the man who was her future, the man who had given her back her son, then blessed her with a stepson she was rapidly coming to love.

Dylan looked deep into her eyes and seemed to understand what was going on in her head, seemed to know that she'd been thinking too much about the past. He intensified his movements, made the thrusts deeper and longer until she could no longer think of anything except him and this burning need to reach some elusive goal.

Then suddenly she was there, her whole body quaking with a climax that drove everything else from her head. Dylan was right with her, too, his timing as impeccable as ever.

Completely drained, she snuggled against him. "Do you think it will always be like this?"

"I think I'll probably die if it is," he said. He met her gaze. "What I really think is how remarkable you are."

"Funny, I was just thinking the same thing about you."

"Which tells me that we're both doing entirely too much thinking, when there are far more interesting alternatives."

Kelsey grinned. "Who needs a honeymoon, when there's a very private jet? Think we can just stay up here?"

"At least until we run out of fuel."

"Maybe we ought to consider getting to a hotel, after all," she said with regret. "As nice as this is, I want to know our future is going to last a little longer than a few hours."

"Your call," Dylan told her.

"Really?"

"Today, anyway."

"And tomorrow?"

"We'll negotiate."

"Everything?" she asked.

"The important issues."

"What about everything else?"

His grin turned smug. "I win."

She leaned down and gave him another long, slow kiss. "You already have."

He gave a heartfelt sigh. "Don't I know it. After all, I've got my family now—you, Bobby, Shane."

She thought of something they'd never discussed, something they should have considered before rushing headlong into marriage. "Do you want another child, Dylan? Our baby?"

He cupped her face. "Nothing would make me

happier. We can have a dozen more, if you want them.''

"One or two ought to do it.''

Dylan's gaze skimmed over her. "Want to get started?''

Kelsey sighed and reached for him. "Absolutely.''

* * * * *

*Watch as Jeb Delacourt tries to discover
if Brianna O'Ryan is the woman to make
him say "I do." Coming in July 2000
from Silhouette Special Edition*

*And now for a sneak preview of
THE PINT-SIZED SECRET,
please turn the page.*

Jeb was a big believer in the direct approach, especially when it came to his social life. There were plenty of people in Houston who thought of him as a scoundrel, nothing more than a rich playboy, who thought he had a right to use women, but the truth was actually very different.

For all his carefree ways, he felt things deeply. Once he had wanted nothing more than to marry and have a family, but now he doubted he ever would. He wasn't sure that he'd ever trust a woman deeply enough to risk his heart. He'd made a decision to keep his relationships casual and his intentions direct. There would be no promises of happily ever after, not on his part anyway. He couldn't see himself getting past his now ingrained suspicions. Of course, Dylan and Trish had felt exactly the same way before they'd met their current matches. Given the family track record, it probably would be wise to never say never, but he knew himself well enough to say it with conviction.

In the meantime, there was Brianna. The very beautiful, very brilliant Brianna. There was no question of falling for her. He already had very valid reasons for distrusting her. Getting close to her would be a little like going into a foreign country with all the necessary inoculations very much up-to-date. But that didn't mean he couldn't appreciate the journey.

After a restless night during which he considered, then again dismissed, his father's warning to steer clear of the geologist, Jeb concluded that the simplest way to discover just what kind of person Brianna was would be to ask her out, get to know her outside the office, see what her life-style was like and if there was any chance she might be spending income that outdistanced her Delacourt Oil salary.

He knew she was single. Divorced, according to the rumor mill, though no one seemed to know much about the circumstances. He also knew she'd turned down dates with half a dozen of their colleagues. Her social life—if she had one—was a mystery. He considered such discretion to be admirable, as well as wise. He also considered it a challenge.

And that was what brought him to the fourth floor at Delacourt Oil just after seven in the morning. Although he knew very little about Brianna's habits, he did know that she was an early riser. A morning person himself, on several occasions he'd spotted her car already in the parking lot when he arrived. Obviously neither of them had the sort of exciting night life that others probably thought they did.

As he walked toward her office, Jeb wasn't the least bit surprised to find Brianna's lights on and her head bent over a huge geological map spread across her desk. Her computer was booted up, and all sorts of mysterious calculations were on the screen.

Since she was totally absorbed, he took a moment simply to stand there and appreciate the auburn highlights in her no muss, no fuss short hair. If her hairstyle was almost boyish, the graceful curve of her neck was contrastingly feminine. She was wearing an outfit with simple lines, in natural fabrics—linen and silk.

"Find anything interesting?" he asked eventually, trying to tame hormones that seemed inclined to run amok at the mere sight of her.

Her head shot up, and startled blue-green eyes stared at him guiltily...or so he thought. Was she trying to pinpoint a new site she could pass on to the competition? When she made no attempt to hide the map, he told himself he was being ridiculous. Any investigator worth the title should think more rationally and behave more objectively than he was at this moment. So far, he had suspicions and coincidence and not much else, yet he'd already all but tried and convicted her.

"You," she said as if he were a particularly

annoying interruption, despite the fact that they probably hadn't exchanged more than a few dozen words since she'd been hired.

"Now is that any way to greet a man who's come bearing coffee and pastry?"

"No thanks," she said, pointedly going back to her study of the map.

Ignoring the blatant dismissal, Jeb crossed the room and perched on the corner of her desk, close enough to be impossible for her to ignore. He opened the bag he'd brought, removed two cups of coffee and two warm cheese danishes. He wafted first one, then the other, under her nose. Though she didn't look up, there was no mistaking her subtle sniff of the aroma.

"Tempting, aren't they?"

She heaved a resigned sigh, then sat back. "You're not going to go away, are you?"

Despite the exasperation in her tone, there was a faint hint of a smile on her lips.

He beamed at her. "Nope." He held out the coffee. She accepted it with exaggerated reluctance, then took a quick sip, then another slow, appreciative swallow.

"You didn't get this here," she said. "Not even the executive dining room makes coffee like this."

"Nope. I made a stop at a bakery."

She regarded him warily. "Why?"

"No special reason."

"Of course not," she said with blatant skepticism. "This is something you make a habit of doing for everyone around here. Sort of an executive-type welcome, a way to let the troops know that management cares. Today just happens to be my turn.''

''Exactly.''

Her unflinching gaze met his. ''Bull, Mr. Delacourt.''

Startled by the direct hit, he laughed. This was going to be more fun that he'd anticipated. ''You don't mince words, do you, Mrs. O'Ryan?''

''Not enough time in the day as it is. Why waste it searching for polite phrases when the direct approach is quicker?''

''A woman after my own heart,'' Jeb concluded. ''Okay, then, I'll be direct, too. I have a charity ball to attend on Friday. It's for a good cause. The food and wine promise to be excellent. How about going with me?''

''Thanks, but no thanks.''

Vaguely insulted by the quick, unequivocal—if not unexpected—refusal, Jeb pulled out his trump card. ''Max Coleman will be there,'' he said innocently, watching closely for a reaction. Other than a slight narrowing of her lips, there was nothing to give away the fact that the name meant anything at all to her. He pressed harder. ''Might be interesting to see how he reacts to just how well you're doing at Delacourt Oil, don't you think?''

''Max Coleman is slime,'' she said at once. ''I don't care what he thinks.''

''Sure you do, sweetheart. It wouldn't be human not to want a little revenge against the man who fired you.'' He let his gaze travel slowly over her, waited until he saw the color rise in her cheeks

before adding, ''You look very human to me.'' He
winked. ''Pick you up at six-thirty.''

He headed for the door, anticipating all the way
that she might contradict him, might refuse even
more emphatically, even though he knew he'd
found her Achilles' heel.

Instead, she said softly, ''Formal?''

He turned back, feigning confusion. ''What was
that?''

She frowned at him. ''I asked if it was formal?''

''Definitely black tie,'' he said. ''Wear something sexy. You'll bring him to his knees.''

Amusement seemed to flit across her face at
that. ''And you, Mr. Delacourt? Will it bring you
to your knees?''

''Could be. I guess we'll just have to wait and
see.'' To his sincere regret, in the last couple of
minutes he'd discovered it was definitely possible.
That alone should have been warning enough to
induce him to abandon his investigation before it
went wildly awry. Instead, it merely increased his
anticipation.

SHERRYL WOODS

*H*eather Reed thought she was making the right choice when she decided to raise her daughter, Angel, on her own. But five years later Heather realizes that she needs help. It's time to track down Angel's fahter.… The only problem is he doesn't know Angel exists.

*I*f Todd Winston is dismayed to see his old girlfriend show up in Whispering Woods, he's horrified when he looks into the angelic eyes of the little girl who is clearly his daughter.

*N*either Heather nor Todd count, though, on their unexpected desire to become a family. The only question: Is it too late?

ANGEL MINE

If you enjoyed what you just read,
then we've got an offer you can't resist!

Take 2 bestselling love stories FREE!
Plus get a FREE surprise gift!

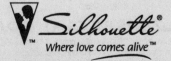

Look Who's celebrating our 20th Anniversary:

Celebrate 20 YEARS

"Let's raise a glass to Silhouette and all the great books and talented authors they've introduced over the past twenty years. May the *next* twenty be just as exciting and just as innovative!"

—*New York Times* bestselling author
Linda Lael Miller

"A visit to Silhouette is a guaranteed happy ending, a chance to touch magic for a little while.... I hope Silhouette goes on forever."

—International bestselling author
Marie Ferrarella

"Twenty years of laughter and love. It's not hard to imagine Silhouette Books celebrating twenty years of quality publishing, but it is hard to imagine a publishing world without it. Congratulations."

—International bestselling author
Emilie Richards

Silhouette®SPECIAL EDITION®

SILHOUETTE'S 20ᵗʰ ANNIVERSARY CONTEST
OFFICIAL RULES
NO PURCHASE NECESSARY TO ENTER

1. To enter, follow directions published in the offer to which you are responding. Contest begins 1/1/00 and ends on 8/24/00 (the "Promotion Period"). Method of entry may vary. Mailed entries must be postmarked by 8/24/00, and received by 8/31/00.

2. During the Promotion Period, the Contest may be presented via the Internet. Entry via the Internet may be restricted to residents of certain geographic areas that are disclosed on the Web site. To enter via the Internet, if you are a resident of a geographic area in which Internet entry is permissible, follow the directions displayed on-line, including typing your essay of 100 words or fewer telling us "Where In The World Your Love Will Come Alive." On-line entries must be received by 11:59 p.m. Eastern Standard time on 8/24/00. Limit one e-mail entry per person, household and e-mail address per day, per presentation. If you are a resident of a geographic area in which entry via the Internet is permissible, you may, in lieu of submitting an entry on-line, enter by mail, by hand-printing your name, address, telephone number and contest number/name on an 8"x 11" plain piece of paper and telling us in 100 words or fewer "Where In The World Your Love Will Come Alive," and mailing via first-class mail to: Silhouette 20ᵗʰ Anniversary Contest, (in the U.S.) P.O. Box 9069, Buffalo, NY 14269-9069; (In Canada) P.O. Box 637, Fort Erie, Ontario, Canada L2A 5X3. Limit one 8"x 11" mailed entry per person, household and e-mail address per day. <u>On-line and/or 8"x 11" mailed entries received from persons residing in geographic areas in which Internet entry is not permissible will be disqualified.</u> No liability is assumed for lost, late, incomplete, inaccurate, nondelivered or misdirected mail, or misdirected e-mail, for technical, hardware or software failures of any kind, lost or unavailable network connection, or failed, incomplete, garbled or delayed computer transmission or any human error which may occur in the receipt or processing of the entries in the contest.

3. Essays will be judged by a panel of members of the Silhouette editorial and marketing staff based on the following criteria:

   > Sincerity (believability, credibility)—50%
   > Originality (freshness, creativity)—30%
   > Aptness (appropriateness to contest ideas)—20%

   Purchase or acceptance of a product offer does not improve your chances of winning. In the event of a tie, duplicate prizes will be awarded.

4. All entries become the property of Harlequin Enterprises Ltd., and will not be returned. Winner will be determined no later than 10/31/00 and will be notified by mail. Grand Prize winner will be required to sign and return Affidavit of Eligibility within 15 days of receipt of notification. Noncompliance within the time period may result in disqualification and an alternative winner may be selected. All municipal, provincial, federal, state and local laws and regulations apply. Contest open only to residents of the U.S. and Canada who are 18 years of age or older, and is void wherever prohibited by law. Internet entry is restricted solely to residents of those geographical areas in which Internet entry is permissible. Employees of Torstar Corp., their affiliates, agents and members of their immediate families are not eligible. Taxes on the prizes are the sole responsibility of winners. Entry and acceptance of any prize offered constitutes permission to use winner's name, photograph or other likeness for the purposes of advertising, trade and promotion on behalf of Torstar Corp. without further compensation to the winner, unless prohibited by law. Torstar Corp and D.L. Blair, Inc., their parents, affiliates and subsidiaries, are not responsible for errors in printing or electronic presentation of contest or entries. In the event of printing or other errors which may result in unintended prize values or duplication of prizes, all affected contest materials or entries shall be null and void. If for any reason the Internet portion of the contest is not capable of running as planned, including infection by computer virus, bugs, tampering, unauthorized intervention, fraud, technical failures, or any other causes beyond the control of Torstar Corp. which corrupt or affect the administration, secrecy, fairness, integrity or proper conduct of the contest, Torstar Corp. reserves the right, at its sole discretion, to disqualify any individual who tampers with the entry process and to cancel, terminate, modify or suspend the contest or the Internet portion thereof. In the event of a dispute regarding an on-line entry, the entry will be deemed submitted by the authorized holder of the e-mail account submitted at the time of entry. Authorized account holder is defined as the natural person who is assigned to an e-mail address by an Internet access provider, on-line service provider or other organization that is responsible for arranging e-mail address for the domain associated with the submitted e-mail address.

5. Prizes: Grand Prize—a $10,000 vacation to anywhere in the world. Travelers (at least one must be 18 years of age or older) or parent or guardian if one traveler is a minor, must sign and return a Release of Liability prior to departure. Travel must be completed by December 31, 2001, and is subject to space and accommodations availability. Two hundred (200) Second Prizes—a two-book limited edition autographed collector set from one of the Silhouette Anniversary authors: Nora Roberts, Diana Palmer, Linda Howard or Annette Broadrick (value $10.00 each set). All prizes are valued in U.S. dollars.

6. For a list of winners (available after 10/31/00), send a self-addressed, stamped envelope to: Harlequin Silhouette 20ᵗʰ Anniversary Winners, P.O. Box 4200, Blair, NE 68009-4200.

Contest sponsored by Torstar Corp., P.O. Box 9042, Buffalo, NY 14269-9042.

ENTER FOR
A CHANCE TO WIN*

Silhouette's 20th Anniversary Contest

Tell Us Where in the World
You Would Like *Your* Love To Come Alive...
And We'll Send the Lucky Winner There!

Silhouette wants to take you wherever
your happy ending can come true.

Here's how to enter: Tell us, in 100 words or less,
where you want to go to make your love come alive!

In addition to the grand prize, there will be 200
runner-up prizes, collector's-edition book sets
autographed by one of the Silhouette anniversary
authors: **Nora Roberts, Diana Palmer,
Linda Howard** or **Annette Broadrick**.

DON'T MISS YOUR CHANCE TO WIN!
ENTER NOW! No Purchase Necessary

Silhouette®
Where love comes alive™

Name:

Address:

City: State/Province:

Zip/Postal Code:

Mail to Harlequin Books: **In the U.S.**: P.O. Box 9069, Buffalo, NY
14269-9069; **In Canada**: P.O. Box 637, Fort Erie, Ontario, L4A 5X3

*No purchase necessary—for contest details send a self-addressed stamped envelope to:
Silhouette's 20th Anniversary Contest, P.O. Box 9069, Buffalo, NY, 14269-9069 (include
contest name on self-addressed envelope). Residents of Washington and Vermont may
omit postage. Open to Cdn. (excluding Quebec) and U.S. residents who are 18 or over.
Void where prohibited. Contest ends August 31, 2000.

PS20CON_R